DISCOMFORT

Design by Brian Conn
Black Sun and Inverted Starfield (cover image) by Jim Lafferty

First Edition
ISBN 978-1-940400-06-8

Ellipsis Press LLC
An imprint of Dzanc Books
PO Box 721196
Jackson Heights NY 11372
www.ellipsispress.com

LIBRARY OF CONGRESS CATALOGING-IN-PUBLICATION DATA

Hampton, Evelyn.
  [Short stories. Selections]
  Discomfort : stories / Evelyn Hampton. — First edition.
        pages cm
  ISBN 978-1-940400-06-8 (alk. paper)
  I. Title.

  PS3608.A69594A6 2014
  813'.6—dc23

                              2014026103

ellipsis
• • •
press

DISCOMFORT

Stories · Evelyn Hampton

MY CHUTE

I would go with my family to the museums and the restaurants, trying to find what I was supposed to love. The nudes were lovely, and I could see how a slab of marble retained the shape of a man, but I would just think how great it would be to have my own chute, a longish tube to push things through — anything, great or trash, it wouldn't matter to me, I would push it all through my chute. It would be easy; my chute would be dark inside at all times of day or night, too dark to see into, so its reality would be mysterious to me — except that I had created it, and knowing this would give me the greatest pleasure because it would be such a relief to look at a thing I had created, which would not exist if it weren't for me, and to see it only partially. It would make me feel mysterious to me. Then I could relax with my family.

But the inside of my chute is not entirely dark. I am not entirely unable to see that my chute now has teeth, though I never intended it to. I had imagined a sleek, nearly frictionless tube accepting of all I pushed through it. I had foreseen the easy slippage of things out of this world, and the spaces, wide and small gaps, that would appear like cats where things had once been, sometimes curling up and warming them.

I had imagined that in the absence of my family, another room would become open to me — the room I had never known how to get to because my family had always been blocking me. With them removed, I would easily enter an area of high ceilings and intrigue. Then my personality would really be free to scheme. I would attend conventions of influence and prestige, where I would be recognized. I would wear a blazer and jeans.

Except that my chute is not at all how I imagined it would be. I can clearly see that my chute has grown teeth around its opening, a line of incisors and canines the size of mine. What is the purpose of teeth if not to block an entrance? I suppose they are also for ripping and grinding. And they hint at speech — they make little walls for words to hide behind before they venture out.

My chute's teeth are not at all useful to me. Times when I want my chute to chew, it refuses. I haul our hideous loveseat out of our living room to the opening of my chute, and my chute, despite what I think it should do, despite what it has done in the past, does not chew. It does not even move (it used to make a worm-like movement that was so endearing to me) to take the loveseat from me. So I sit on the loveseat beside my chute, bored, barely different from being ordinary.

At these times, the only difference between me and someone who sits on a loveseat in front of a TV is that I fed my TV to my chute. I wanted only my chute — I needed no other images than it. I imagined it and then I made it, and when it was made it was no longer part of me. Yet to see outside of me something that had once been part of me was not as entertaining as I'd expected it would be. In fact it was very lonely. I discovered, once it was made, that my chute had had a hidden use — it had kept me company. Imagined but still unmade, my chute was always with me; I could push anything through it; in fact my chute was the end of all my senses — whatever I heard, felt, saw, touched, tasted, or thought, all could be pushed into my chute, leaving me clean, my senses fresh, as if unaffected by anything. I could push my family through my chute — my chute was very accommodating. Whatever I wanted to lose, there my chute would be, moving like a worm, taking it from my hands, taking it away from me.

3

During the time when my chute was real only to me, my chute and I shared the same body. Our blood circulated in my veins. What I ate kept us happy and the same.

Then my chute was finished. I had needed to make it in order to feel entirely real. As long as I couldn't see my chute — as long as it was inside of me — I couldn't know for certain that my chute wasn't just a feeling — insubstantial, made of the chemicals of my brain. Even if a doctor could have shown me an image of my chute, still, I would not have been satisfied.

But then to have my chute removed, to have it entirely outside of me —

my family arrives in the Subaru; its windows lower automatically; they look at me; they look at my chute; they look disgusted; they are on their way to the museums; they are condemning me by looking at my chute —

has been my greatest failure and, I realize now that it is real, my greatest fear.

•

How to get my chute back into me? — I write this on a piece of tissue, then push it into my chute.

4

My chute is suspended at one end from a platform in a tree. My father built the platform for me — I had told him I needed to be able to see (in fact I faked a kind of blindness until he built the platform for me).

My chute angles sharply away from the platform, down through the leaves of the tree, to a place on the ground I prefer not to acknowledge.

I have come to believe that my chute is growing — not *growing away from me*, but growing actually, quantifiably. I have taken a tape measure from my father's hands and I intend to measure my chute. I intend for my measurements to be accurate, exact, but my chute does not make precision easy. By its nature (now that it is out of me, my chute has its own struggles) my chute defies precision and accuracy. It goes off into the trees, suspended every few feet by thick straps tied to branches, toward the source of a river we are forbidden to touch for it has been polluted by us.

My chute does not even move to take the tissue away from me.

My chute is no longer mine.

I would like to convene a meeting concerning my chute; I would like all to be in attendance, especially people with excellent minds; at this meeting the agenda will be *How to get my chute back into me*. I believe this will be a great scientific and philosophical challenge, in fact the greatest of our time, for my chute challenges a duality we have yet to resolve — *thoughts* and *things* are names for two sorts of object, which common sense has always found contrasted.

Now that my chute has become a real chute, how to get it back to being imaginary and mine? It is obvious that this implicates both space and time.

I will need the greatest minds, those that still hoard their excesses, their deepest mines, keeping them unbuilt, undiscoverable — not suspending them stupidly from trees, not exposing them to the eyes of their families.

I shimmy along the outside of the chute, stretching the tape to take measurements I record in a notebook I am quickly filling with questions and observations about the chute. I would record equations, too, except that I don't have any yet —

it is obvious that the chute is growing, perhaps toward a point that is dimensionless —

though I expect to, soon.

THE FOX AND THE WOLF

I would take the things that had no power of their own into my plastic play home. It was there that I pretended to be a woman. I was hungry and bored by the story of the fox and the wolf.

I had things I pretended were remnants of a future I had yet to inhabit: branches of dogwood; carcasses of dead birds, squirrels, chipmunks; the limbs of my brother's plastic figurines.

Using a watering can, I could fill these remnants with what filled the faces of our neighbors when they heard their proper names called out. It was very bright and could not be eyed directly. My ability to do this was often questioned from a window of my parents' bedroom.

As a child, I thought the future promised this: God and some disciples come in a van and they fix the parts of the landscape that we used up and eroded when we were desperate and unaccountable even to ourselves, and we are accountable again when the landscape is restored. So much of what we were depended on the upkeep of the land.

My family had problems that were caused either by my parents' ineptitude or someone else's, or neither, or both. I didn't feel like a girl, and I didn't feel like a boy. But I had been named and the name took on the shape I grew to inhabit.

I often didn't immediately recognize them as my parents when I saw them from a distance, or when they were standing in a place or a way I hadn't expected to find them. I was assigned the role of the father when playing house. The plastic play home would bend and change shape when the sun weakened the internal structure of its walls.

I did not question how much I loved money. I thought it was beautiful, and that its absence was the bank's beige waiting room when I was hungry and lightheaded and my mother was hungry and lightheaded and she would tell me, Sit still and read the story of the fox and the wolf while I talk to someone who will help us.

From where I sat waiting, the back of her head was certainly someone else's. On the other side, I expected to find a stiffly painted expression that mirrored the stiffly painted expression of the man or woman who sat on the other side of the desk.

The future I had yet to inhabit was everywhere filled with the satisfaction of the purchase of the plastic play home — the moment when authority relents to my wishes, it's sunny, I'm at the top of the plastic play home's tower, I can do anything, I'm in charge of the ones in charge, God is a melting plastic figurine in the grass, sun makes the plastic tower curve softly, I'm getting too heavy for this play home — but it was an unreliable satisfaction: the soft parts of my body were smooth when we were wealthy and rough and sweaty when we were poor. They were so changeable, and I began to mistrust them as I would another's body.

In the story of the fox and wolf, one always knows just how to manipulate the other. The manipulator is always punished.

Sometimes, especially when we were poor, it seemed that the landscape was more crowded and difficult to pass through. Some part of it would snag on us; some part of us would break. We would have a flat tire because someone had strewn nails on the highway, and we would buy milk that smelled like the dogwood did in the spring, when it festered with stunted worms, and something alive was dying in the gutter. Something seemed to want to punish us, and when we were punished, we wanted to punish other people. When we were poor we would call the neighbors more often for help, and we would say, Hey Bob Gary Susan, could you? Often it was my mother who called for favors while Dad mended his ladder because when we were poor, something always seemed to be up there on the roof in the gutters clogging up our lives.

When we were poor Dad tried to fix his ladder. When we were wealthy he said, To hell. To hell with that ladder. I'll just hire the kid to come and unclog us.

The kid came with his own ladder and crawled up onto our roof and unclogged us. While the kid crawled above us, Dad would be nodding into his book. He often read books by men. Yes, very good, he seemed to be approving, by way of the book's author, the kid's work, which was an indirect approval of his own work, since it was Dad's work that gave him the money to pay the kid.

I wondered, When we were wealthy, was every book Dad nodded into an indirect approval of our family's happy economy? Because when we were poor, he would pick up a book, put it down, pick up another, put it down, and so on, unable to read, and mutter, and look out the window, and shake his head. Hell, hell, he would say, and we all had bad haircuts.

The fox would win because the fox could read and thus became clever. The wolf could only read certain words, such as its own name. The wolf was vain, and in children's stories one is always punished for vanity, usually with ugliness and exclusion.

I braided my own hair by reversing my thoughts about my body. I unraveled my name by writing it over and over, forwards and backwards, sensing the oddness that goes into and comes out of language — how the word ENTER on the revolving door of the bank only seemed spooky when we were out of money: ENTER, seen every which way, was awfully close, in my desperate mind, to RENTER, which (Mom said "God forbid") we would never be.

There was also the appearance of our last name in cursive on the mailbox in which we would find threatening, desperate, insulting and untoward language — *Delinquent, Canceled, Never, No, No love* — some of which I had written and addressed to myself out of boredom with myself.

The fox found out the wolf's hovel, and when the wolf was out hunting the fox, the fox laid a trap in the wolf's hovel.

We were most of the time average, but sometimes we were poor, and sometimes we were wealthy, and less of the time we were very poor, and even less of the time we were very wealthy. This left us in a Rambler with a sloping yard heavy on all sides of us, and on all sides of our yard were neighbors with stern, empty faces that filled with something anonymous when we called their names: Hey Bob, Frank, Marlene, Betty, Hey Jake, Chris, Sarah, Emily, Hey Susan Thomas Gary Henry Hey Mike and Adam. It was like their names, hunks of bread off some common loaf, filled them, and made them alike and happy.

As it turned out, the hovel where the fox laid its trap was not the wolf's only hovel; the wolf had many hovels, many ways to conceal its appetite.

At night, standing outside my plastic play home and looking inside our Rambler-home, I could see Dad rubbing his hands together outside my bedroom door. Read the story of the fox and the wolf quietly to yourself and then turn out your lights, he must have said to my closed door. He looked hungry. Once — we must have been poor — I watched him eat an entire loaf of bread by tearing hunks off and stuffing them into his throat.

The wolf had a bad reputation for tricking little children and for always being hungry. I knew this from other stories. Still, I often sympathized with the one set up as a bad example. I was often hungry.

We were most of the time average, and this average way of being arranged the landscape so that most ugly things were hidden from our eyes, and most nice things were just out of reach, but many good, reliable things could be purchased in the Red Owl or the

Rainbow or the Target. These colorful places gave objects lore and mystique and a kind of inner movement that made me want them uncontrollably.

The landscape, the one we could afford to inhabit, was mainly flat, with a few hills built by tractors for sledding, and ravines dug by diggers for taking away things that had no power of their own, and many, many lakes that concealed the small lives shifting beneath their surfaces. There were many such surfaces. I wanted to touch beneath them. There was something that I wanted that was there, but I didn't know how to just grab the thing I wanted. This not knowing how to just grab the thing I wanted, which seemed to be everywhere and nowhere, created a tension that appeared in me as bad moods, tantrums, irrational grievances, petty theft, addiction to candy, uncertainty, poor math skills, and occasional child-on-child violence in unteachered corridors and playgrounds. I preferred to fight beneath slides, where the sand was always shaded, moist, dark, and absorbent. I thought I wanted the braids of the blond child, and so I grabbed them. But the braids screamed, and I was punished. And so on. Things were taken from me in several swift movements.

A swift downward movement: something was removed, a block of my tower, so that the tower tilted and what once held the tower up was broken. No efforts were made to rebuild the tower, no, no, leave me alone, I hate those books, I hate this, I hate you!

"Go to your room."

The girl was taken to the top of the tower by an unseen upward movement, hunger. A fox and a wolf were preparing a meal in the kitchen. The wolf asked the girl, "Why is your dress so filthy?" The fox said, "Leave her alone, can't you see she's hungry?" The wolf said, "That's got nothing to do with it! I'm hungry too!" The fox said, "Oh, you're so stupid. Why do you make things harder for yourself, for us all?" The wolf backed into the corner the refrigerator made with the wall and touched a coil of metal, and the fox called her bank account by angrily pushing buttons recessed in gray plastic.

The girl was seen fleeing the tower in the direction of a neighboring tower, knocking on a door, running to the next tower, falling down, knocking, crying, and so on, down the block of towers —

"You're too old to be doing that!"

Another swift movement.

Something else is taken away.

In this way, through a series of swift movements, each movement taking something away, I aged.

EEG

Grandpa had his funny EEG machine hooked up. On its green screen, my mind was several colored lines. "I'm going to ask you a few questions," he began. "The questions are as follows: What is your name, how old are you, and what is your earliest memory."

Grandpa was a psychoanalyst. Then he got equipment and could watch brains flicker on a little green screen, so he switched from being a psychoanalyst to being oddball, Grandma said, but lucky for him, by then he was retired. Sometimes also he would go out and take pictures. He had a dark room where he would show me what he'd been.

"This is my first wife," he said. The photo hung above his and Grandma's bed. Grandma was in the kitchen, picking up knives. The first wife still occupied the house.

What I'd been trying to do then was to collapse everything onto a single, flat surface. I wanted to see what would happen if many people occupied the same face.

Another time I was trying to work from within objects. If there was movement, I wanted to show the molecules around that movement. If Grandpa stood near me while I painted, I would paint the awkward distance between us. This is why my faces kept cracking open. I was interested in observing what happens at the surface when one is under extreme pressure.

.

That winter, the lake was frozen October until June. On the green screen, I saw how my brain behaved like shattering glass. Each time I blinked sent a spike to my brain stem. This was what was missing from all my portraits, then: all the interruptions caused by blinking. "Each time you blink there's a small fit of activity in your brain," Grandpa said, "like a table cloth being pulled from under set dishes." He always liked to explain. Anything, he would try to explain it. His EEG was portable so he could bring it to the kitchen. Grandma didn't like it. "You want to see what my brain looks like when I'm sharpening knives?" Grandma had her privacies. When a window frosted over, she'd shave the fuzz off with a butter knife. I tried to show the blinking and all those interruptions. I put the paint on so thick it had to crack to dry. All those cracks would look back at me, reflecting light at different angles. Those are the kinds of faces I wanted to see.

At night, I walked out onto the frozen lake. I wanted to go under and see a flash of something. When that happens to a person, their life can't escape from that moment. Everything collapses to a point. It happens like a tic. It had happened to Grandpa after they crashed. When he looked over at his first wife, she didn't look back. The highway had crumpled up their car like it was a first draft. His face began to tic, only on one side. He got the EEG machine to try to find out why. But all the lines on the still side spiked and sputtered like normal. The disruption was somewhere else. Maybe it would always be where he wasn't looking. Still, he kept her photo above the bed and looked from time to time.

·

"Look at that!" He was pointing out the window to the darkening sky. A bird or something above the lake. I hadn't seen it. When I painted his portrait, I painted Grandma's meat cleaver inside his forehead.

"Wish I'd had the camera," he said.

Grandma had all the knives sharpened by breakfast, so I painted the knives during the dull hour after. I showed them in a line on the counter, with Grandpa's hand on the counter too, and the lines of the EEG machine running beneath it all.

.

"Electrical activity gets more regular when you close your eyes, unless you're imagining something gruesome," he told me the first time he hooked me up to the EEG. I wanted to paint the insides of my eyelids the same way I'd painted the knives, from inside. But I hadn't painted the knives yet.

When we all sat at the table, we sat on different sides of the same brown line.

"Things in your world can't hold anything or be held by anyone," Grandpa said. "You give them such flat, bright light. But my world includes shadows," he explained later in his dark room, "so it's easier to inhabit, because there are places to hide. See? Where are my hands in this picture?"

.

Grandma wanted to cook venison for dinner. The knives were sharp. But Grandpa was missing. She needed him to bring her the venison from the deep freezer, so she could start it thawing in a bucket of water. The deep freezer was the shed down by the lake. I told her I'd go and get it.

When I got to the shed, I saw the shape of Grandpa by the edge of the lake. I called out to him. Maybe he'd decided to wait for the flash of something he'd seen earlier over the lake. Well, except he wasn't moving when I called him.

·

"Think of something bad, think of someone slowly climbing the stairs with a knife behind his back," he told me. "Who is he?"

I tried to think about what he told me while I watched the green screen. It was difficult to think of something besides the lines that told me I was thinking. The light blue line was my brain stem and the red line was the front of my brain and the brown line was for tying my little boat to the dock. I thought of those lines flattening out, or becoming twisted into a braid. How would I get them untwisted? When I spoke, the lines got twisted, but they untwisted as soon as words were off my tongue.

"You're still young," Grandpa said, "your mind is nimble and quick."

Then he said, "Is it me? Did you think of me with a knife behind my back?"

·

When I called him and he didn't look up, I felt the lines twisting into a hard knot, a thought.

He'd dropped through the ice to his knees. Shock stopped his heart. I couldn't haul Grandpa all the way to the house to Grandma when she was expecting venison.

"When you're in a relaxed state of expectation, the waves in your brain are quick and rhythmic. It's rare for the parts of your brain to be this willing to cooperate with one another. But as soon as something happens, they will be divided. One part will help you immediately react, and one part will be working out an intelligent explanation for it all ..." I don't remember the rest of all Grandpa told me. I broke up the ice around him with my hands. I got him to go down.

THE LARGEST UNOBSTRUCTED AREA
GIVEN TO HAM

For Dennis, no thoughts came from ham. For Sean a little thought, a miniature ham. It sat on a miniature plate, but then it started to be a hat, and soon a man was wearing the hat and telling Sean to eat the ham. Without identifying him as such, Sean knew the man was the Commander, and that the hat he wore would never go back to being the miniature ham, which had been so good to Sean because it had looked just like the ham he was about to eat but had also been small enough to fit whole inside his head, and its wholeness had consisted of various scenes from the past three months of Sean's life of Sean successfully leaping over large holes of known area but unknown depth that Dennis had created.

If there's going to be a plan, it has to come from inside Sean, Dennis thought in momentary lieu of a bite of ham. Only Sean knew that inside Sean the Commander wore a hat that had once been a miniature of the ham Dennis was now large-scale eating. A series of joins between disparate entities and experiences connected the men to each other; for Dennis the series of joins was visceral, transitory pleasure enduring now as ham; for Sean the series was a more static structure, a house situated on what happened when Sean thought the words "arable land." When Sean thought about its construction, the house would lose parts of itself inside itself. Nevertheless, lately Sean had begun to inhabit one of the lost quadrants of the house.

In the lost quadrant Sean had begun to inhabit, Dennis ate ham and Sean tried to diminish the Commander by thinking "arable land, arable land." A notable feature of the Commander was that he was Sean if Sean were to wear a hat that had once been a miniature ham and now cast a shadow the size and shape of the average-sized ham Dennis was eating, Dennis being an important structural element of the house that was for Sean what gathered and held in coherent order all that connected the men. Sean believed that Dennis received experience through a filter or screen that corresponded to an object Sean often encountered in his dreams — a telephone. Dennis believed that he received experience via the ham and Sean, whose face formed part of the background of the ham. Sean, now that the comforting thought of miniature ham had become a commander he had to combat with "arable land," tried to find some comfort in the thought that he, Sean, was receiving experience by way of the dream phone — that it was all a message being relayed to him by someone else, a dream interlocutor whose important role in Sean's life could only be known when Sean situated himself in one of the lost quadrants of the house.

"Arable land, arable land," the voice on the other end of the telephone was saying, and this voice now belonged to Dennis, and was Dennis's only voice within the house. But the voice was something additional, an overlay of voice atop the underlay of voice that was actually Dennis's, and it confused Sean, why Dennis was introducing this unnecessary technique of asserting his authority, using the dream phone to say the words that were what the house was situated on — they were its foundation.

So now that Sean's plan came from Dennis, and Dennis ate ham, Sean ate a bite of ham, connecting himself, for Dennis, to Dennis. Part of what formed the background of the ham, for Dennis, was Sean's face; the part not formed by Sean's face was a window, and through the window Dennis saw the tinted window of a van. Though Dennis could not have known this, the tint of the window was the color of the phone through which Dennis's additional voice repeated the words that had been Sean's private command, or anti-command, since they opened up space that had been occupied by the Commander and his commands to Sean to eat ham.

"Arable land." Sean ate ham. He and Dennis ate ham together. For Sean, this shared act of eating ham became part of the structure Sean had recently begun to inhabit, and for Dennis, this shared act of eating ham was a shared act of eating ham, one with a foreground (ham) and a background (Sean's face, tinted window of van), with Dennis positioned at the shared act's center.

NOWHERE HILL

There was a particular place in a particular park where a person could stand, at a certain time, on a certain day, and cast no shadow.

I happened to be in the park within an hour of the time on the day when a person could stand in the place and cast no shadow.

It wasn't the place that cast no shadow, but the body that stood there, and though the body stood there, it would appear, because of the place where the body was standing, and when the body was standing there, as if nobody stood there.

The place where a body could stand and cast no shadow was called Nowhere Hill.

An older child who had a way of holding a ball close to his body while he was running that we all admired and tried to mimic, that older child was the one who said he would be the one to cast no shadow when the time came.

He was wearing a watch.

I was also wearing a watch, but I had decided to hide it.

I had decided to hide my watch, so I had taken it off and put it in my pocket, where it didn't feel like a watch anymore, and it didn't look like a watch anymore.

I had decided to hide my watch because I thought it would be safer somewhere hidden, where the other children could not see it, and not seeing it, they couldn't break it or take it away from me.

Hidden inside my pocket, the watch felt like a heaviness in my clothing, like sweat, and while I was aware of the heaviness that wasn't sweat yet felt like sweat, the heaviness wasn't uncomfortable. Yet it didn't bother me until I began to think I could detect an odor coming from the heaviness.

I was running alongside the other children, following the boy we all wanted to follow, to the place where he would stand and cast no shadow, and I became aware of an odor coming up through my clothing from the pocket I had put my watch into, to hide it.

Could my watch be sweating, how else could it have an odor, and other thoughts I tried to push away as I continued running alongside the other children, running through tall grass, wanting to arrive, after the boy, at the place where he would cast no shadow.

But it wasn't even time yet, we were early, I knew, by half an hour, yet I didn't want to take my watch out to check the time because now I was certain that the watch had a terrible odor that was polluting the insides of my clothing, an odor that would seem to the other children to be coming from my body.

If I took the watch out of my clothing, it would pollute the outside of my clothing, and since outside of my clothing was everything else, including the children racing alongside me to the top of Nowhere Hill, I couldn't take it out of my clothing because I didn't want to pollute them, I wanted them to accept me as someone to run alongside in a race to the top of Nowhere Hill.

It was important to me that we were running together, that we wanted to get somewhere together, and not running because we wanted to get away from someone or something. Running to get somewhere together was my favorite way of running, it was exciting, the place where we were all going was special because we were all going there together, it didn't matter who got there first because what mattered was that we were all going there together.

Running away from someone or something was frightening because you were alone even when you were running together, running together didn't matter, you didn't know where you were going or whether you'd be safe when you got there, worst of all was to be the one the other children were running from.

So I at first didn't take the watch out of my pocket because I didn't want to pollute the outside of my clothing with the odor and become something to run from when what I wanted was to be someone to run alongside toward the place where we were all going, the top of Nowhere Hill.

And I was running fast and by now breathing too hard to be able to coordinate the watch's removal and the reading I would have to do of its hands and numbers.

It was a Mickey Mouse watch my parents had given me.

Mickey Mouse's hands, in those big white gloves he was always wearing, were what told you what time it was, even in the dark, because the big white gloves could glow in the dark.

When they glowed in the dark, the big white gloves were not white but yellow, yet still big, these two big yellow gloves pointing in the dark at different parts of the dark where you knew numbers were, but they didn't glow, so you couldn't see them, but you knew the numbers were there like faces whose voices you know so well you can hear them even when they aren't there.

Running, and smelling the odor that came up through my clothing, I thought, It must be the gloves that I am smelling, the odor must be coming from those gloves, Mickey's hands must be sweating and making the terrible odor.

I pictured the big white gloves that would be yellow in the dark of my pocket, two big yellow gloves pointing at different parts of the dark in my pocket where I thought the watch would stay hidden, but now I understood how it couldn't stay hidden because of the odor coming from Mickey.

Now that I had thought about Mickey's hands sweating inside those big white gloves — were they big white gloves or big yellow gloves? — those big gloves, I couldn't just keep running, and though we were nearing the place where the boy would stand and cast no shadow, I had to stop because Mickey's hands were sweating inside his big gloves inside my pocket and I didn't want the other children to think that it was me they were smelling, that the odor of Mickey's sweaty hands was the odor of my body.

No.

I stopped running.

I took the watch out of my pocket.

I looked at the watch.

I looked at Mickey Mouse's skinny arms, which I now hated because they were connected to the hands that were sweating inside those gloves, which stank, and whose odor had contaminated my clothing and now everything outside of my clothing.

I looked at the gloves and could see how horrible they were.

How horribly big they were compared to the rest of Mickey's body, what terrible thing they might be concealing, that Mickey might be concealing, to be sweating such an awful sweat, to be making such a terrible thing with his body.

Up ahead, in front of me, up the small hill, the other children were playing with each other, pushing each other's bodies away from the boy who would soon cast no shadow.

And their bodies, too, seemed terrible, they too were part of the way Mickey's sweaty hands were pointing at two different things that meant the same thing—the time, but really it didn't mean anything, just some number—because they occupied the place where Mickey's terrible hands were pointing, the place where the boy's body would soon cast no shadow.

Now the boy and the other children were counting down, chanting numbers until the time when his body would cast no shadow.

Eleven, ten, nine ...

I could feel the sweat on my body cooling.

It would be easy to do and I would do it.

Eight seven six, they were chanting.

Standing at the top of Nowhere Hill, the boy appeared tall because of where I was standing, yet because of where I was standing, at the bottom of the hill, in grass that was tall, with a thing in my hand I no longer minded losing, that no longer seemed worth having, I no longer cared where he was standing at all.

They said the rest of the numbers, and when they said zero, the number that meant nothing at all, I threw the watch as far as I could in a direction I would never go to retrieve it, I threw the hideous creature in the horribly big gloves and I didn't care whether or not they were white or yellow or whether he cast a shadow as he got farther from me and I got farther from Nowhere Hill.

BOY

He'd found something blue to use as a voice, and soon the entire sky was implicated by him: there were no edges to its or his accumulation. For a time in the presence of what I took to be his mood, I was confused — uncertain what was or wasn't an aspect of his identity, I thought everything was or wasn't, a back-and-forth of consecration and profanation that included in their extent the realm of all things and all people, living and dead. And so at both ends of my existence I butted up against him, and unable to live or die I became a thing that only slowly, after much time, is no longer associated with any idea. As an artifact of a time in which I had lived, I did not live, I persisted — if form were given to what I was, that form would coincide precisely with Earth's revolutions, and from a space dislocated from ideas I would appear no different from any mystery caught in the pull of another mystery's gravity.

It was only by persisting in uncertainty and confusion that I came to resemble what is human. Life had in its manifold an impaction, and that impaction caused a series of events, one of which I was, and later, so was he. But he, I sensed, was some aspect of me, a projection of my most disparate elements, so he was in every sense a contradiction. Every day I struggled to make sense. I had blisters where each foot rubbed against the shape of what had been made to contain it, yet wanting an even more visible manifestation of containment, I wished my whole body would swell with irritation at the rules and procedures into which I had entered by becoming human. It was all too much to do: eating take-out chicken and watching the news while maintaining my belief in the uncategorizable source of my and everything's existence. One night I ate spinach Florentine while the news showed a picture of the universe taken from a place inaccessibly beyond it, and overwhelmed by the simultaneous possibilities and restraints of existence I demanded of the absence behind the camera, "What am I supposed to do!" Immediately nothing happened.

But soon he'd appropriated blue as the primary way his voice would come through, and then even the most ordinary things seemed to have ulterior attributes — the true function of a chair was totally beyond my idea of what a chair could do, and there was nowhere that I could rest. Nothing I could eat would satisfy my hunger, which also seemed untrue. I had many things to do because I lived in the city, and I had a pressure behind my ears that was aggravated by enclosure, elevators and subway cars, the cupping of hands to block out noise. My clothing was tight and I was in a hurry, but because of the pain I was in I had to move slowly, taking the stairs and walking. Maybe by being slow I was predisposed to him, slowness being one of his conditions, and approaching my true existence from a distance far beyond what I could travel, I felt my blazer loosen. Knowing I would never reach my destination, I soon had little to do but look for him.

.

So, slowly, he emerged from the conditions of my existence — not much work, hardly any money, bread that came wrapped in plastic and was the same all the way through. By way of a sequence of days, anything that strayed into my field of vision — all the extrusions of lights, signs, buildings, and people among which I lived — took on a life separate from mine, and a meaning other than any I could provide. High above the city one night I looked down to see the still center I rotated around. Carnival music blared to conceal the groan of a motor much older than the view it afforded of the city. There were so many separate lights — which was mine? Or was mine what kept them separate? At a certain point he was just there, living among the lights and what separated them.

One morning, a curtain hung in the window of a dark cafe the way vision would persist for a time after I closed my eyes, so I closed my eyes, and then he came. But he was not a surprise. He became himself so gradually, it is hard to choose one moment as his first, as his —

band of light coming through the window, band of light no longer coming through the window —

he entered the space between two incidents as a bar of music coming through an open room. At first his presence caused me pain — he, like a phantom limb, was a phantom identity. He did not yet have a body, so his presence was like a body in a dark I could not illuminate. I did not see him or hear his voice, yet there he was, behind sounds or between them, behind lights or between them, recognizable through his way of entrenching himself. I sensed that his appearance, when it finally came, would be the disguise of unknown laws and forces that he would coerce me to name.

I tried to escape what I expected of his rage — I went back to taking the subway and drinking coffee. My outfits became a mix of stains, rooms in hotels all over the city, the clashing brocades of where I stayed because I didn't want to go to my apartment. I knew he would be there, reading something vague about the urgency of appearance that he would try to explain to me, and I did not want to hear it. There was enough else that was vague — on the news the universe had become smeary, and we were only shown what the president could see, and who was he? Sometimes we got to see him the way he saw himself, a smooth, competent talker who looked and sounded like his father, who looked and sounded like himself. Other times just faces floating, disembodied: a desert, then a quick flash to cowboy boots that became John Wayne. In the president's dreams, when he did dream, we would see the violent scenes we had heard the news wasn't reporting, but then these too would get blurry, and a harried, suited woman would appear as if it would be worse to be reassuring.

At the office, I positioned myself between two machines, one for receiving what the other would send away. Both were familiar and beige, emitting the heat of their beeps. I was there to maintain their familiarity, making sure that everything was received and anything strange sent away. Sometimes, between them, exhausted, I would sleep. When there was a jam in either the receiving or the sending away, a path of blinking lights that would eventually lead me back to the machines was illuminated for me. I knew that I too would eventually be sent away, or I hoped I would be, or I thought something likewise vague. Though I might like to have changed everything — to have packed practical clothes and gone to a more straightforward place — the means by which I might make a change seemed distant, or no, not far, but connected to him, and he was connected to me by a kind of flesh that he was using me to make.

Come out of my mouth, I said to him. What I ate, I fed to him.

.

It was slow, but once the process of making him had begun, it advanced. Though I call it a process, it was not anything I have ever known how to structure or control. As he claimed them for himself, I would see objects from my past in a quick flash. One day I saw a dress on display that I immediately desired to own. By its color I knew it was something I had been as a child, when my sense of self was a condition that arose from a color my mother would paint on my toenails, *Dusty Rose*. Hers was an aesthetic of silence — to paint small surfaces so lovingly, and to paint nothing else. Through her, I knew no other fate than a gradual appropriation of matter. Swallowing long strands of her hair that had broken off in the hotdish, I picked at the table's finish and felt full when a long stripe of something clear came off. Together we would take refuge in an ever-fading, ever-renewable set of attributes and the feelings they conveyed by way of color and sheen. Yet within the assemblage that was my identity then, I began to feel a rot; something trapped by lacquer had begun to fester. When I managed to contort my body in such a way that I could touch what I thought was the source of the rot, what I touched taught me to shave.

What I began to call *boy* was my separation from a life and meaning that were not mine. It was not that I desired a release for sex, a pet — I had never wanted one of those. And my desire to have a child had subsided long ago. No, by separating my life from one not my own, there was less and less I desired to possess, and as I desired less, he claimed more of what I had seen and known, reaching from the present far north, into my past, pooling in the source my father once insisted we cross so as to alter the river's flow.

It was the day I saw that dress, the words *Dusty Rose* escaping its folds as if language was matter's echo, that I decided to appropriate silence — he had taken nearly everything else. I studied how silence subtended itself. I found all around me an envelope of silence — if all of existence could cast a shadow, that shadow would be the realm of existence itself, I thought, but soon gave up thinking about silence so as to live in it. Words that had always seemed encased in useful, familiar shapes came up through surfaces as if objects were disgorging unwanted content. One night as I turned off the light in my bedroom, I watched *bedroom* debride itself from my small attempts at decoration. I slept in a nameless, empty space I was waiting for him to fully enter.

As more and more words abandoned their objects, something strange happened to space: walls, doors, partitions, thickets, every kind of boundary gave way. Though I could still see these things, they meant nothing to me, and I inhabited space uncontained. Since my body's boundaries meant little to me, morality also meant little, and the boundary between the holy and profane went away. Something seemed about to matter, something I had forgotten about to be remembered. That summer the air was hot, a film of lust collected on it that at night was projected onto a screen. Sitting among many others, I watched those images for him.

OFFICE

Yesterday in my office, I read an article about elephants in a zoo that spent long days of an unusually hot summer lying in the sun, refusing to go near a small pond that was filled by a cascade of falling water. The elephants' handlers would try to bribe the elephants with treats to go into the water because they feared the elephants would die of dehydration. Nothing the handlers tried could coax the elephants into the pond. Instead the elephants drank hot water from a small plastic trough the handlers placed beside them in the sun. Finally one day a hard, soaking rain began to fall, and all the elephants got into the pond and played beneath the falling rain, sucking water into their trunks and shooting it at each other, splashing their enormous bodies in and out of the water.

Today I went to the pet store and bought an aquarium and two turtles. I bought all the accoutrements for the tank and turtles, and now in my office I can watch them swimming in a small pond and perching on a stone, sunning themselves beneath a heat lamp. For me, having pets is a novelty. I wasn't allowed to have a pet as a child. Now I can spend hours in my office watching the turtles. Recently I noticed something strange about them. After I had siphoned dirty water out of their tank and before I siphoned clean water into it from a large bucket I keep on the floor, the turtles crawled to the glass wall of their tank and peered down. I watched them doing this for a while and finally understood that they were looking for the source of new water as if to inspect it, to make sure of its purity before it entered their home. When I understood that they were doing this, I positioned my face so that it blocked the source of new water, forcing the turtles to look at me. The turtles soon turned away and went back to the warmth of the stone beneath the lamp.

·

I don't think the right sort of work for me is studying animal behavior, yet I keep thinking about the way the turtles turned away from me. I want to come to some general conclusion about the turtles and what they want in their lives that I can apply to me and what I want in my life. *Self-referencing is the mind's tendency to locate*

itself, so when it's realized that there is no self apart from the perceiv-
ing, the tendency to try to find one's self in any experience, insight, or
concept, ceases, according to a book I've been reading in my office.
The book was written by a monk who has stayed in one place for
the past forty years examining the ways his mind forms attachments to its own ideas and images, which he calls his self. Images
and ideas carry with them a kind of space unlike the space that
surrounds real objects like turtles and stones and the knickknacks
that crowd my desk. If I could get rid of the knickknacks, I might
have space in which to perform some sort of task, but since I don't
know what sort of task I want to perform, I don't know how much
space I'll need, so I keep the knickknacks on my crowded desk.
Besides, during this time when I have not yet decided on the sort
of work I will do, I like to look at my knickknacks and consider
the few that are still mysterious to me. One of these mysteries is
a spiky brown pod attached to a small branch that at one time
must have been attached to something larger, but having broken
off the larger thing, now it is here on my desk. Spikes cover the
ball, which several days ago developed a small crack that has become a large crack. It's the sort of enlarging that comes before a
hatching, I imagine, and I imagine that something will crawl out
from the crack in a few days to ask me difficult questions that I
will not be able to answer. I imagine that what crawls out will be
the monk.

Another of the mysteries on my desk is a rusted mechanism
that looks like a small wheel inside a bracket. There are holes

where screws could be inserted into the bracket and the mechanism attached to something large and stable, like a house or a monk. There is a final mystery — two nameless birds depicted on a round coaster, the sort for putting beneath beverages. The birds are illustrated in a style familiar to me from a book on the history of scientific illustration that I have been reading in my office. The coaster is one of two that I've had since I was a child: on one, there is an illustration of a flower, and on the other, an illustration of the two birds. I do not know what kind of bird these are — there's no name below them like there is beneath the flower, which is named *Viola odorata*. The surface of each coaster has been crazed by age and heat, and I realize each time I look attentively at the crazing how comforting it is to be able to see the things around me aging. I have a sense of my own aging though I can't see it, yet it seems right that I should be able to, that the surfaces of my eyes should craze from exposure to light and heat and the unexpected things I've seen, and that I should have to see after a while through an expanding network of cracks and crevices that grow wider and wider until eventually one crack is the size of a door into which I disappear. But there is only a gradual blurring in me as I get older, so I am glad to own a few things where I can watch happening on their surfaces what I would like to see happening to me. The two unnamed birds are perched on a stylized, gnarled branch, as they were when I was a child, and for the past twenty years the net of cracks in which they have been caught has been emerging from the white background, pushing through the leaves and the white vacancies between them. If the birds were to try to fly, they would find this net prevents them from gaining any distance from the positions in which their illustrator has depicted them.

A couple of days ago I was paging through the book on the history of scientific illustration, and I came across the same illustration of *Viola odorata* that appears on the coaster on my desk. According to the book, the *Viola* was included in a treatise on medicinal plants by Serapion the Younger, a physician, in AD 800. His work was transcribed by a monk, Jacopo Filippo, in the 1390s. Yet it's not known who illustrated the original treatise, I read, sitting in my office, and I began to feel satisfied, then self-satisfied, with this bookish not-knowing, a feeling that, as soon as I became aware of it, prevented me from reading any more that day.

·

Once, a physician showed me on an ultrasound the empty shape of my uterus. When my boyfriend and I have sex in my office, his sperm swim through my vagina and cervix into the emptiness. I imagine the black and white screen of the doctor's ultrasound while my boyfriend's body moves with mine and against mine. Sun reflected by the yellow house next door shines as yellow light into my office, and it is in this yellow light that I think these black and white thoughts about my body. Though I could imagine the interior of my body in any way I wanted to, the way I do imagine it is just like what I've seen on the doctor's screen, which seems like a trustworthy intermediary. If I could see what was happening inside me directly, I'm not sure I would want to look.

People have been trying to see into themselves and the things around them for a long time. In the book about the history of scientific illustration, which I am reading again, there's a diagram that a hunter in the Northern Territories of Australia has scratched of his prey, a kangaroo, into a piece of tree bark. In the diagram, the body of the kangaroo has been divided by lines into quadrants representing its bone structure and possibly organs, though it's clear that these have been imagined and not seen firsthand — the kangaroo's belly is filled with a fanciful latticework of diamond shapes, and the rest of its interior is divided geometrically into shapes like triangles and quadrilaterals. Beside the kangaroo, a stick-figure hunter crouches with his spear. His erect penis is enormous, half the length of his leg.

When we moved into our apartment, I painted the walls of my office a color named Eggshell. I have begun drawing on the Eggshell walls in pencil at night when the streetlight casts shadows into my office. It's difficult to see these drawings unless you're looking very closely, and even then the wavy pencil lines look more like cracks in the walls than anything deliberately drawn. I've begun thinking of these drawings as "night murals." Sometimes I trace my own shadow, sometimes the shadows of other things, sometimes the shadows cast by the irregular surface of a wall upon itself. Many previous tenants have painted the walls of my office, and these layers of paint have built up like strata of earth over time.

From my office in the evening, I look at the sky in the spaces carved out by the columns of the neighbor's porch and lose track for a while of everything's size — the carved-out spaces are the same shape as the spaces between the slats of my father's chair back, the chair he would sit in to read to me from books about faraway places, some real, some imaginary, and I think of all the places I've never been that I'd like to return to in an impossible body — the body of an unnamed bird or a spiky brown ball — places I've seen from far above, or passing fast. Traveling through the Alps in France, I looked down and saw a tiny village in a valley nestled in the cleft of a river's path. A precarious form of life completely dependent on a thing as capricious as a river — I think I could be happy being that.

·

A few days ago in my office, as the sun was going down behind the columns in vivid pinks and reds, I read that often what complicates the diagnosis of a disease are the many kinds of bacteria the environment of the disease becomes host to. The article showed a photograph taken through a microscope with polarized light in which each strain and species of bacteria was a different neon color against a vivid pink background. The caption included this caveat: "False color is frequently added to monochromatic micrographs by computer processing, and in many such modern images the information content becomes secondary to the vividness of the result."

I have been reading a lot, trying to figure out what sort of work I want to do in my office, yet the more I read, the more I wonder how much of the information I come across I can trust. It seems that so much of what people do is unintentional, and open to interpretation, that even after I have amassed a lot of information, I will still have to figure out for myself a way to order all of it; otherwise, lacking a coherent structure in which to fit the interesting things I find out, I will forget them, or I will believe something false, or something injurious to myself and others. I've hung a photograph in my office of German bathers at a public bath. The photograph was taken from above, the point of view from which it's apparent that the people in the water have arranged themselves (without, I assume, planning to) in the lattice structure of a crystal. I've read that a crowd of people moves around obstacles just like flowing water. I've read that when there's limited information about where resources are located, people tend to move in patterns that resemble waves. I've read that each person, by thinking only about her or himself, contributes to a pattern that may be unrecognizable to the people the pattern includes, and I can almost start to believe that what appears to me to be chaotic is actually the orderly functioning of an organism much larger than myself, and which I am one small part of. At Ohio State University in Columbus, Ohio, pedestrians have walked their own, more efficient paths among the concrete sidewalks that have been laid, creating an interweaving of paths that is geometric yet informal. I've hung a photograph of these paths in my office beside the German bathers. The paths wind along and crisscross an oval of green grass, creating a pattern remarkably similar to the pattern on the shell of one of my turtles.

Sometimes I read and sometimes I look at the turtles, but mostly what I do in my office is think about what I would like to be doing in my office. When I make friends online from a computer in my office, it's with the belief that the more contacts I have, the more lives I will have access to, and the more lives I have access to, the more advice about offices and what to do in them I can solicit. But more information is not necessarily going to lead me to make the best decision, and it may be that I'm not any more likely to figure out what sort of work I want to do in my office by talking to people I barely know about the sort of work they do in their offices; maybe I'll be more likely to figure out what's right for me if I talk to nobody, or only to a small group of people, my family and neighbors, for instance. From my office, I can see into a small, office-sized room of my neighbors' house, and when I look into this room I see my neighbors sitting in the flickering light of a television. I know that watching television isn't what I want to do in my office, so it seems useless to ask these neighbors what work is right for me to do in my office — unless they can recall having seen something on television that might reveal my work to me. I know that neither my mother nor my father has ever been in my position — having an office but not knowing what sort of work to do in it — and that if I were to ask them for their advice, they would tell me things like, *Your generation has too much time on its hands*, or, *When I was your age*, and so on, and I would never get them to sincerely attempt to address my predicament.

Possibly, I would be better off not having an office until I decide on the sort of work to do in my office. It might be best for me to spend my unemployed days wandering my neighborhood, following established paths and creating new ones, and watching traffic as it passes. I would be an exile from my office, and in general I think an existence of exile would suit me. I don't really know who I am, and I can never feel settled. When I come home after a day of being out, I feel sad, as if something that never had a chance to begin has ended. In my office, I have tried to think about my origin, but the place I come from — the roads through it and the roads leading up to it — seems nondescript and vague, without clear boundaries, and I don't really know how to think about something that seems limitless. Looking from where I sit in my office through the columns of my neighbor's porch and seeing at the same time through the slats of my father's chair, I feel that I occupy two times at once, and since in each of these times I have a body, I also occupy two bodies at once. It's an uneasy feeling, so I sit very still, uncertain which body will respond when I next decide to move. Yet I am finding I don't mind this uneasiness — I think I am good at tolerating it, so I wonder if this could be the work I should be doing in my office: sitting still, feeling uneasy and uncertain of which body, in which time, will move when I eventually get up to go to the bathroom.

I have never been good at knowing where I am, but when I was a child I didn't know this, and believing that I knew which room of my house I would be looking into at the top of my climb, I began my way up the trellis in my mother's garden. I was startled when what I saw wasn't the sink and dirty dishes in the kitchen but my mother's naked body reflected in the mirror of the bathroom. Surprised to see my face suddenly next to her body in the mirror, my mother screamed. This startled me again, and I fell down into the roses, crushing them. It wasn't the first time I'd seen my mother naked — the sight of her body hadn't startled me because it was naked but because it was in the bathroom. Had I seen her naked in the kitchen, the room I'd been expecting to find, I doubt I would have been so surprised.

Among the night clouds, the brightest spots are the windows of churches — there are so many in this town, and rather than be inside any of them, I'd like to stay outside of them all, where it is dark, and where the light in their windows shrinks, momentarily, the hugeness of the experience of night to the size of a window frame, a human labor. I begin feeling at ease, and soon I am not by myself anymore but walking with a friend. She is back from a trip to some faraway place, but instead of telling me of the strange things she's seen and done there, she tells me something ordinary, and as she speaks, what she says isn't separate from the light coming through the windows above us: she seems actually to be admitting light to me, as if she has always performed this loving labor. If there could be more of these transparencies, and friends to make them, not just windows but new forms, ones that bend out of the familiar gradually throughout the day so that as the day is darkening we begin to see them — then loneliness might become a discipline like architecture, and students will travel to cities famous for their loneliness, and at evening these students will go out on solitary explorations and gradually see, bending out of the storeys of buildings, the intricate fretwork of their own experiences.

I haven't told my boyfriend about my night murals — I think they would make him uneasy. He's already uneasy about the walks I've been taking alone at night through our neighborhood, which many of our neighbors believe is becoming less safe. After his bicycle and kayak were stolen, one of our neighbors began locking his new bike and kayak to a frame in the bed of his pickup truck. Even in winter, when he pulls his truck out of the driveway, it looks as if he's going to the beach for a weekend vacation. Walking around our neighborhood at night, I don't feel threatened by things outside of me but by things inside of me, which flicker and take different shapes. Sometimes the shapes are familiar — people I've known, things I know I've seen — and sometimes they are strange — unknown and frightening. There was a day last week when I woke in a terrible mood after dreaming of a door through which I could not pass though the way wasn't blocked — there was something else preventing me. I spent the day in my office brooding over the little tasks I'd set for myself—changing the water in the turtles' tank, reading from one of the many books I've begun but can't seem to finish—without accomplishing any of them. Finally I began to feel less oppressed as the sun was going down, so I left my office and then the house.

INTERRUPTIONS

She calls me late at night. Her way of talking to me is to find me in my sleep, then tell me things I don't want to know.

Hello, I say. I hear the sleep in my throat. As if my throat is the path sleep travels to my head, I swallow to keep it out.

I hear a train where she is. Her voice and the sound of the train come through together, but neither comes through completely; some of each stays inside the sound of the other, or is cancelled out by the other.

She lives in a state people talk about as a place that's flown over on the way to a destination. Though cancelled out is not the same as never having been.

I want to tell her this: earlier today I was in the garden digging a hole, and at the bottom of the hole I saw translucent beads that I thought was a necklace without a string. I thought of a woman, and I said, Some woman ... A man who was also looking into the hole said, Those are a slug's eggs. He suggested that I stomp on each one to be sure I had destroyed what was inside, so I did. I stomped eleven times. Then, with a shovel, I made another bottom for the hole, and I didn't find any more eggs. A hole can have many bottoms, as many as you want to give it. That there can be so many makes the hole bottomless.

I know she's going to ask me to stay with her. She is always asking me to do things for her. I don't want to go to her state to be with her. I want to stay in my own state where I can watch container ships go out into fog and return carrying fog's products. In her state, trains carrying the containers that ships bring to my state's harbor don't always stay on their tracks.

I haven't been sleeping much, she says. Can you stay with us for a while?

Another train is in her voice. I think of the straight tracks in her voice, and of the more complicated places where the tracks curve and overlap to allow the train to switch to other tracks.

Never mind, she says. I know you're busy.

But still, she says.

It's a long train that passes.

I'm still not used to these interruptions, she says.

I think of steel curving in the darkness.

.

She was married one December.

I wasn't at the wedding. She is my sister, but when I say the word "sister," I don't think of her. I think of an off-white sheet that has tiny stains on it that look like tiny flowers, irises and roses. When I admit that she is my sister, I'm saying that she gives me the flowered sheet to sleep on when I visit.

We don't look alike. We don't talk alike. We don't move our hands in the same way when we're telling a story. We don't tell the same sorts of stories. She was born to our parents after our father was sick with something he never named and never let out of his body. He let it out into Mom and made me, she says when she's feeling sorry.

That is her sort of story.

.

When I am flying through darkness toward her, I look out of a window.

Do you think the slug remembers or senses where it laid its eggs? I asked the man when we looked into the hole.

The man sitting beside me on the plane grabs for the plastic arm-rest between us at the same time as I am grabbing for it.

I don't think a slug has any way of telling its eggs from another slug's eggs. Or any means of caring whose is whose, he said.

We end up grabbing each other's hands. We each let go quickly. We land.

.

Weeks that I am with her pass, bringing more weeks in their wake.

When I go outside of her house and stand on the concrete bottom step, before I step off of it, I have the feeling that I want my body to be carried off by whatever is mobile.

I direct my thoughts at the upper branches of trees, at the places where a wall meets a roof, where a gutter meets the sky. The place where a deer emerges from the forest on the other side of the rail-road tracks is made distinct from the place where the deer reenters the forest by the way the deer moves through it. Though the location might be the same.

I watch a train pass.

Actually, I watch it pass piece by piece, as much of it as I can see at a time. Because I can see only a little at a time, seeing seems like an interruption. I have to put the whole train together later.

.

Some people say they can tell an empty car from a full one, she says later.

It's night and we are in her kitchen. Her son, the one she calls troubled, is asleep. We can hear his head banging on the headboard.

Outside, a train is passing.

Why does it make that rhythm do you think.

Ker-thunk-ker-thunk-ker-thunk.

The son she does not call troubled is the troubled one's twin.

I can't tell which is which just by looking at them.

We know that the troubled one is asleep because we go into his darkened room and balance a glass of water on his chest.

They say the empty ones rise off of the tracks a little. The full ones keep the empties from flying off.

It's only when we are out of the room, in the kitchen again, that he begins the rhythm again.

It's worse than ever, tonight, she says.

If a person behaves like a piece of driftwood in an eddy, if a person behaves like a piece of trash caught in the spokes of a careening vehicle, held in circulation of a momentary center, I wonder what I have been looking at lately to want to make such comparisons.

Lately so many train cars have been empty, she says. People can't afford the things they used to carry in from the edges of the country.

The son who isn't called troubled tells us he's going for a walk.

.

In my dream, I talk to him. He looks like the place where the deer reenters the forest when it's startled.

I kneel there, in the place that's for both emergence and reentry, wanting to ask it a question, but my thought is interrupted by morning.

.

At breakfast, I ask her, Where were your sons born? I can't remember.

She asks, Who were you talking to in your sleep?

I'm home, says the one who isn't called troubled.

An orange peel on a plate fools me, I think it still holds fruit. I reach for it, then stop reaching when I figure out that it's empty. The rest of the reach is an empty hand in my pocket.

She asks him, Where is there to go all night?

Are there any more of those oranges, he wants to know.

·

Look, she says when the troubled one is in the shower. She makes a motion that means I should follow her into his bedroom.

I see where he's worn a place in the wood of the headboard. It's the repetitive movements of his head against hard wood that have made a smooth, concave place. I put my hand there. Then I take my hand back.

It's as if he's digging a hole with his head, I think. A hole through the headboard, then maybe he'll begin digging through the wall. Then I think: A head shouldn't be used this way — why has he decided to use his head this way?

I'm sorry, I say.

There is soft tissue between the pieces of the skull, though covered in skin and hair, they appear fused.

·

Plates, they call them, she says to the troubled one when he peels his orange onto the table.

.

A train derailed last night, the one who isn't called troubled tells us.

Eighty, ninety cars.

Which one? asks the troubled one.

I couldn't tell in the dark.

LOOKOUT

I grew up feeling that there is an emptiness in what is apparent that needs to be filled by accounts from witnesses we can trust. As this feeling called into question the mechanisms of vision, the visible portion of me began to diminish, and if I was noticed at all, my mother was admonished for my paleness and uncertainty. I ate constantly, yet I remained only marginally part of the visible world. Asked a question, I'd shimmer the air to show I was there. *Here*, my mother would say, holding out a pat of sweetcream butter. But I felt unsatisfied by anything presented in the form of a solution or cure. I remember having passed through a door one day at school and, expecting to find myself in the restroom, finding myself instead in a courtyard where a man and a child were laying tiles in a complicated pattern that extended in all directions farther than I could see. Nervously folding a used tissue, I thought the pattern might make visible the limits of my body, so I tried to include myself in its permutations. I wanted to understand where I was in relation to where the pattern began and where it would end. Could I lie down among its repetitions and feel included in infinity? *Causes are inextricably bundled*, the child started to tell me. Yet I longed to be satisfied by ordinary things like my mother and sweetcream butter.

Four walls of windows, gaps in chairbacks, cracks between doors and their frames — our tiny house did little to contain me. I felt all around me the presence of an arrangement that connected with my body yet remained out of reach. I ranged along the periphery of the forest my mother, the lookout, watched for fire, breaking off leaves and flowers for later identification, nibbling what I knew I could safely eat. I had a facility for names and relations, something orderly inside me. I quickly learned all the names there were to know in the forest, yet as the presence eluded each of these, I began to doubt any satisfaction I might get from my ability. I lost focus, left home, went to where the land was vast and open, where I stayed for many years, moping. To all who saw me during those years, I was hardly there: I appeared as though another object's shadow, and my presence could only be perceived by way of a feeling of uncertainty about which was more real, the object or its shadow.

Now that it detects a threat along its periphery, the government decides it needs people like me — a relief to my mother. I am given a job in a temporary security-seeking administration — temporary because we are working toward our own obsolescence. Most of my work is done along the periphery of vision, a region of dense fog that threatens our sense of security even as it confers desired privacy. I buy a house in the city and invite my mother to move in with me. After years of being a lookout, she is exhausted yet still vigilant, her eyes perpetually in a squint. She's the first to notice me when I'm home for a late-night supper.

I can remain withdrawn from visibility for hours, but hunger still brings me into my mother's kitchen. I put thick slices of Munster on a plate with rice bread and grape butter and carry this to the porch, where my mother perches on a high-backed, narrow chair she swivels with one foot. "It's been a busy night," she says, and I take it that she's referring to my work. From her perch she can see the light in my office, which, from this distance, is a stand-in for me. That it's still on means I'm still working, I won't be home for long. "There's the report on the efficacy of the police," I say through a mouthful of cheese. She smiles — deep wrinkles around her eyes and in her cheeks. As lookout, she's seen better than anyone the corruption of the police.

"Did you — oh good," she says when she sees I've found something to eat. Though we're both physically slight, beside my mother I feel sprawling, sloppy — she lives so neatly whereas I range in and out of boundaries, searching for what I don't know the name of, constantly doubting my ability to find it. Why not live simply, not question the efficacy of the police, the solutions and cures presented to me? But that question is outmoded by my mother, the things she sees and what knowledge of them does to me. I eat constantly, gaining little; doctors suggest a dissipative digestive disorder, energy lost to unknown processes. Because of processing and preservation we can eat the same foods regardless of season, yet convenience does not necessarily mean comfort. I feel churning in my stomach and doubt whether I should have eaten so much grape butter, one of many food products that is always cheap and available yet not satisfying. Instead of finishing my dinner, I perch beside my mother, looking for an alternative to grape butter, which may come from the trees that grow beside the river, a place I have not explored because it is supposedly dangerous and dirty, the source of the city's corruption, and concealed by the fog that forms at the limits of vision.

"Going for a walk by the river," I tell my mother. I know that whatever she says, she'll say it warily, a cage she puts around me out of habit. But she is distracted from me by something I can't see or don't notice, and she swivels toward it, away from me as I leave.

.

I wander through corporate infrastructure toward the river. The parking lots are empty, yet fluorescence continues to brighten their immensity almost to its landscaped hedges, where differences between nature and artifice are obscured by a darkness that is more like absence of fluorescence than its own presence. I find a path between the hedges and step among piles of garbage, a mix of synthetic and organic, one often containing the other. I crush a Styrofoam container and it is filled with dead leaves.

I have to remain marginally part of the visible world to maintain my job and identity, but at times I long to merge with something inevitable and large — join a flock of migrating birds or condense into a cloud. When my mother first spotted corruption among the police — off-duty officers taking bribes from defense attorneys, subsequent dumping, in the river, of evidence — she didn't tell me or anybody. "When people feel safe, they don't want to question what makes them feel that way," she said. As what she'd seen overwhelmed her other senses, she developed an inability to taste.

I was never good at cooking or cultivation, but I began doing them anyway, hoping to find a flavor she could sense. I took time off from the office and built beds where I planted garlic, onions, radishes, peppers — I hoped she'd taste their strength. I planted mustard greens and endive, hoping their bitterness would float up through what she couldn't describe except by analogy, pointing to a shadow of a useless object and saying, "It tastes like that." I planted basil, oregano, thyme, savory, arugula, sage, mint, rosemary, hoping one, or a combination of some, would correspond with a dish she once ate, and that through its memory, her sense would renew itself.

She ate white beans with spinach and sage — "Italy." She held a bean on her tongue — "Yes, the Florence Cathedral, its dome."

Slowly, she regained taste as heightened ability to see. I tried new combinations and she saw what was hidden in them. Though she had retired from looking out for fire to live in the city with me, she went back to looking, perching on the patio, accepting little to eat, seeing what was invisible to me. It was she who noticed cops making late-night trips to the river, and because of what she's seen, though my job was to monitor the periphery of vision, I changed my focus to what was apparent, happening right in front of my face, and began collecting evidence against the police.

·

At one time, I thought science was a way to see without need of a body. Though I would like them to be, my observations are never completely empty of me. Now I am interested in that irremovable bit of self. I empty my pockets of the seeds I gathered yesterday from landscaping between corporate office parks, fill them with the fallen leaves and fruit of trees I find growing by the river — not a kind I know from the forest. In my office, I'll look carefully at the leaves, observing their pattern while my mother looks out for me. In the fog and darkness that now surround me, the feeling of my mother's eyes on me acts as my vision. *I know my mother is watching me* is my experience of this city.

.

Back at my office, I find my father has arrived ahead of me. He likes to stop by at night when he's off-duty — he's the sheriff's deputy. He doesn't know about my investigation; so far it has yet to implicate him. He sits in a corner watching TV, a show that exaggerates both the effectiveness of the police and the nature of crimes actually being committed. We see a high-speed chase — we don't see the effects of the city's noisome drainage, or unfairnesses in zoning. He loves the show about police. He pities whomever they chase.

I should finish my statement, but as long as my father's here, I know I won't be able to concentrate on it. He talks to the TV when the police speculate about motives — "Darn right he's guilty" and "just look at him." He leans forward to see more closely the blur that conceals the face of the handcuffed man.

I empty my pockets onto my desk and examine my cache. I like how it looks, this little pile of fruit and leaves — it reminds me that I can gather what I need, I don't have to accept what's given to me.

While the police threaten a masked man for the camera, I bite a piece of fruit, hold the pit in my teeth. Then I notice ants, almost too tiny to see, crawling on my desk, crossing from where I can't see them, through visibility, and on to where I can't see them again. In the brief space where I can, I wonder where they come from, what they eat. I imagine living beyond the limits of vision, in microscopic communities, my life just one of many structuring the visible world.

JULIAN

It took Ruth a long time to begin seeing Julian. At first he didn't
have the shape of a man, but of the piles of furniture and clothes
she'd see heaped beside the road. He leaned the way an old mat-
tress leaned against a tree. He moved like a curtain that had been
pulled across a window just when she'd happened to glance at
it, as if the curtain had been animated by her glance. At first,
the way wind blew empty cans across concrete was how Julian
moved — erratically, surprising Ruth sometimes by his sudden-
ness. But soon he could soothe her too, like when he moved by

pushing himself gently along the horizon, filling and emptying the sails of the boats that stayed far out in the bay.

It became easy for Ruth to keep making him this way. She would do a little each day, adding to and taking away from who he had been the day before. She worked at night before her eyes got too tired to see who he was becoming. She would take what she'd seen on her way home that evening and add it to him. A silk dress would lend itself to his skin. The trees, their grays and greens, these would get into his eyes. How tall grass lay flat after it was cut would become his hair. Faces she'd seen reflected in windows would have a way of becoming his face, overlapping him. The way a man she'd passed had been clasping his own hand, as if preparing to ask a question, this would become one of Julian's mannerisms.

She put everything she could see into him. Even her own reflection was there, and the square of the mirror that showed it to her, and the crack in the wall behind the mirror, and the wall: it was all there in Julian — if she looked at him long enough she would see it all.

Sometimes she thought she might be making him too beautiful. A cloud could become him too easily. The way rain gathered and ran down a windowpane in a slow, continuous stream should not be the way he came into the room, so easy it was like falling asleep to watch it happening. So she would take the rain out of him but leave the windowpane, only she would put a crack in it; or she would leave the rain but take away the pane, so when the rain came in she would get wet. She would put night into him in-stead of evening, when the sky was too pretty anyway. She would add to his face the darkness that accumulates in corners and the interiors of inanimate things — to the pupils of his eyes, the spaces between his teeth.

She knew that inside Julian an interior was accumulating and taking on a shape. Sometimes it seemed vast and steep, like a canyon, and sometimes it was a nearly flat cavity, no deeper than the space between wall and mirror. Other times it turned and furled like steam rising from her mug of tea. Other times, it was a shell's spiraled cavity. And yet other times she had no idea how deep it might be. These were the times when Julian was the most real for her; appearance pressed flush against actuality and he would come to her bed and stroke her hair and tell her what he had done that day. He would say something plain — "I went to the post office" or "I picked up some groceries." She would listen closely to the sounds that came out of him, trying to imagine the shape of what was inside him. Do you love me, she would sometimes say, but this was just a way of learning about the shape — did it go on indefinitely? What color was it? Was it gray like the clouds she'd used to add shadows to his face? Did it have many parts, cham-bers, like a heart, or was it a single space? Was it contiguous, or were parts of it cut off from the others, sealed away, unreachable and silent? Did it have thin, delicate parts that were stirred by any disturbance, like the field of wheat she'd seen and so had added to Julian the way it had swayed?

No matter what Julian answered, each time she would hear the shape differently. Do you love me? — His answer would come by echoing, so she thought the shape must be huge, cavernous, nearly too narrow to pass through, then opening into a vast chamber where ferns grew toward a few rays of sunlight. — His answer would be flat, a piece of paper slid across a desk, a contract. — His answer would bounce around, changing shape as he spoke, and she would think it must have come from the street, where kids were playing basketball and cars passed fast with their radios on and windows open. — His answer would be slow to emerge from anyone Ruth brought home.

MOLE

I recently embarrassed myself among savvy friends by showing surprise at the fact that sperm determine the sex of embryos. I had thought they only made males. You knew that, my boyfriend said, looking at me sternly. No, I didn't, I said later when we were alone outside the restaurant.

I am not surprised when everyone around me seems to take more interest in sex than I do. It seems that sex is something that people are naturally drawn to — they like to watch images of sex moving across screens, and they like to talk about and enact those images with other people.

On the night of my recent embarrassment, we were having dinner at a sushi restaurant known for its high prices and accommodating wait staff, who gladly lie across patrons' tables to serve hand rolls and sashimi off the exposed parts of themselves. Our dinner companions, a couple, have been trying to conceive. They both want a boy, and they both have many ideas about how they can make this happen. Supposedly, a boy becomes more likely when a woman is inseminated when she is close to ovulating. Girls are caused by yogurt. No yogurt, our friend says. Absolutely none, says her partner.

I eat yogurt every morning for breakfast. It is one of the only things I do regularly. I rarely have sex because I don't like it. I just don't know, I tell my boyfriend, maybe try from the other side?

·

A close friend from childhood who's now in medical school is fascinated by all that can go wrong in sex and reproduction. Recently she sent me this email:

> Subject: Complete hydatidiform mole
> It means to be pregnant without an embryo. There is only a placenta filled with water. Somehow, when the sperm fertilizes the egg, the genetic material from the mother is lost. Then, either the sperm divides so that there are two pronuclei that fuse to form the nucleus of the new cell, or another sperm fertilizes it.

My friend has told me that she loves having sex. She is married and still can't get enough of what she loves. A few weeks ago she confided in me that she has been having an affair with her body buddy, another medical student she shares a cadaver with. My friend said that many long nights spent dissecting a dead body with another person lead inexorably to sex. Maybe you should try it, my friend said. She added, We do it with the cadaver in the room.

I have never really been interested in sex or reproduction. In high school, I was a good student except in biology classes. Biology teachers never seemed to like me. It was as if something in them was repulsed by something in me. It occurred to me one day in the class of a particularly hostile teacher that it might be something evolutionary, that maybe there are some people who are genetically predisposed to hate sex and everything that has to do with it, and as most of these people don't reproduce, there are fewer and fewer of them. Maybe I was one of a dying breed. Whether or not it's true — now I feel silly even to admit this, since of course hating sex might not be genetic — I still believe that something like this might be possible, and that eventually, all of the people alive on the planet will be the ones who love having sex and babies.

I have met other sex-haters, though it's rare to find them. And it isn't even that we hate sex; we're simply indifferent. I've found that people who actively hate sex tend to have a lot of it, violently, with whips and other implements for torture. I have had sex with one, and while it was interesting for a while to watch the hatred move around behind his face while he contorted his body and mine into different grueling positions, I eventually got bored and soon stopped seeing him except in dreams, where I sometimes still see him, though it isn't him so much as the hatred I see moving furtively behind thick trunks of deadened trees in pursuit of me.

But indifference is something else. It isn't the terrifying subject of nightmares but a fact of everyday life for me. It is, like yogurt, my regular thing.

For a while I dated someone who, trying to entice me, would buy me tea. He would pay surprising amounts to have dried leaves shipped from places too remote for me to remember the names of. Usually the packages came scrawled with Chinese characters over which a small label would confer a few words of poorly translated English: *Beneficial for her abdomen*, and *Take morning for night with mild water*, and *Narrow leaf for her interest to drink*. This boyfriend also wanted me to make certain sounds over and over. He found a mantra online that he said would have aphrodisiac effects. I made the sounds every night hundreds of times. I just want to go to sleep, I finally said.

Since sleep is a nighttime alternative to sex, I have done a lot of sleeping, and in my sleeping, a lot of dreaming. But dreams do not feel like other people. I keep running and running through those trees not knowing why they're all dead, and in the morning, when I wake beside another person, I am uncertain what, and how much of it, can be said.

My current boyfriend says that he would like to have children — maybe three. A boy, a girl, and the third could be a surprise. I do not want to have any children, though I wouldn't mind being pregnant with water. To carry a placenta full of water, even to give birth to a small amount, a cup or two cups — that thought comforts me. I have always liked being around water.

When I imagine giving birth to a human baby, I am filled with a great grief, and something without an end begins to unravel in me.

.

I suppose it's sad that, not enjoying sex, I've lost an important way to connect with other people. Maybe I feel a little more separate and a little less happy because of it, but I know that I am also not happy having sex.

I am happy when I am walking alone along the narrow path above Cape Perpetua, a foggy outcrop of mountainous, forested land that in photographs appears desolate and remote, which it really is. I've come here by myself for a vacation and also — my boyfriend doesn't know this — to search for a place to live.

I'm worried about you living there by yourself, my friend emailed after I'd sent her a photograph of the cape that I'd taken from the cliff above. *Where did you say this place is?*

There's something I've found here that's unlike what I've found anywhere else, and I wonder if it approximates the intimate connection people experience while having sex, when the sex is the sort that unifies two people so that they seem to inhabit a single body. I have heard sex described like this, and though I have never felt this unity while having sex, I feel it when I'm walking alone above the cape, looking down a steep drop-off of hundreds of feet to the tide pools and wet debris of a stony beach — I feel that I am two of something that has finally found a single body.

I told my friend not to worry about me, yet I wonder whether she really should worry. Walking above the cape this morning, I wasn't worried about myself because I didn't feel that I had a self apart from the cape to worry about. To worry about myself living alone on the cape would have been to worry about the cape living alone on the cape, and where else would a cape live if not on an oceanic coast, where rocks are constantly being pummeled and tossed by waves that are sometimes the size of houses, sometimes even larger?

Sometimes the water is calm, I replied to my friend.

GIRL

There's nothing about her curls that I haven't seen elsewhere in the world — I've watched streams and been caught in them. The way steam leaves a source of heat is one of the many ways to leave that I'm familiar with. People talk about life's mysteries, but I've seen clouds from above, and descending through them, I've looked up. Yesterday, I found one of her gloves — wind came and filled it in. With wind I put my fingers in — gloved, my touch resembled her touch in that it no longer felt like anything. Numbness doesn't bother me — silence at my nerve endings connects to wider silences, and I move through these as I do through memories of feelings, heedless of whether I still have legs. A river is known to grow opposite its flow, its water extending from stone — I go in and out of the dark, one of dark's many mouthed and hairy parts searching for its other parts. I find an auditorium just before music starts — I know the just-before part intimately since it's come to be the closest I can get to release. I follow tracks in snow to a burrow — in the dark opening I see the hollow inside her sleeve as she'd reach for me, for some other part of me, a part I now can't see. Maybe at the beach I'll see a wave curling toward me, and if I swim out a ways, maybe looking back I'll see the backside of its shape, and there she'll be, looking the way she used to look when she used to sleep next to me. Asleep on the train her body would sway — drowning must be the way she dreams, I'd think, or from dreams, drowning the way she wakes. But she could find me even in her sleep, and in my sleep I'd begin to have legs, and I'd dream them, and soon the space between them would come into my dream — sometimes a blocked road suddenly opens, and turning down it I find it isn't a road but an omen. Her hand moving up my legs, finding the place where legs become a single leg. Once we were there, where the light was beaconing. I stood still on the stairs while she ran ahead of me — I wanted to see her spiraling up and away as if she were the still one and I was sinking in one of her drowning dreams. I had always thought I'd make a noise, some sound of me I'd later find surrounding me. Or I'd hear it coming from some boy while he pounded me, pushing his body toward whatever he found in me. But what came instead was rain.

Though this event might be the one by which I eventually explain why she left, I find only silences when I try to explain. The most I can do is show you those, and maybe, by way of the contours of things, you'll be able to see how it was. It was messy, our food stuck to the rug. Each new thing that stuck became an obstacle to what at the time it was still fine to call *love*. I would have soon said *fuck* had she not left before then. I had a rash that hung open when I was on top — I used it on her the way she used her underthings on me to get her off. I'm not sure what it was I was getting her off of — off of me, sometimes off herself, but also off of something other than us, some star far from those claimed by constellations I can name. Her light absorbing and re-emitting mine — I don't want it to turn out that with her, I was by myself entirely. In her I don't want to find my mind, my way of worrying about time. For instance, I worry that the passing of it leaves only memories, and that in mine, I will be all I can find. At least now when I look I still find more than me — the time I watched her running away from me and felt I'd lost my mind, but had lost it so gradually that, now that I knew it was gone, I had no idea where to look for it, and if I looked, what I'd find. I look for the parts set back from the other parts, as if a doorway might show me what I'm trying to say besides that it's shadowy, or a window might give way to another way, one that precludes all this trying to explain. I said I can name, but I can't name any of it — star, or gathering of stars — the little twinkle children sing. Children who name even invisibilities would soon have some name for me, or at least some way of telling me apart from other nameless things. I watch a woman being handed a bag for which she pays, and there's something about the bag, maybe that it's opaque, that seems much better an answer than anything I can say. I see the same bag caught in a tree, wind filling and emptying its shape, and my argument — not one I make, because it seems already made for me — is complete. So, since the argument has been completed for me — by what, the economy? — I don't have to say that she worked at night and so did I, and we would meet on the morning train, and I'd watch her sleep and sway until the morning I saw her on the other train going the other way. Maybe I was still sinking and she was reminding me. All this superfluity — I could begin again, go around the other way, and in so going find those ideas about reversibility that fail when applied to time. I wonder, if I could no longer see the openings to places she might be, whether she would come to seem less real to me, being sealed away? Or would the sealing become a dumb spirituality, something I couldn't say so decided to venerate? Maybe better not to say, but in not saying, not to praise. I put my hand in her one glove and don't look for the other one, letting my other hand go numb. I've heard numb's a way of making yourself come — the difficulty is to sustain the numb to some end, or at least release from wanting one. It's possible, she said, to kill a thing so slowly that in death, its life continues unchanged. And so I am thinking about what I did yesterday and what I'll do again today.

MY FEET

When I try to explain what has happened to my feet, I look at other parts of me — my hands, knees; I look in windows when I pass them and hope to see what I need. What do I need? A way to speak about my feet. What's important about them can't be seen, yet walking past a seafood restaurant, I look in the window and see a woman sitting at a white tablecloth cracking the leg of a crustacean. I think it refers to me — the cracking, the crustacean: the entire scene an indication of me. As if the world were nothing more than my indices. But the woman doesn't notice me; and I am inventing these indices, inventing *me* in order that you can understand my feet. I cannot feel my feet, though doctors say they are perfectly healthy. They have the sheen of healthiness — well-fed flesh, soft and warm and clean. They appear to be a healthy part of me, yet I cannot feel them. This affects the way I walk particularly, but also the way I see and speak, since when I see my feet I can't believe them, and when I try to tell someone about the discomfort that has replaced them — pains that resemble different edges: serrated, hooked, razored — I resort to describing the qualities of other objects, not my feet.

But — "cracking," "crustacean": these words have qualities that might tell you a little bit about my feet.

And even though speaking is often useless, I feel a compulsion to speak about my feet. Especially while I am walking I want to be talking about my feet. I think I can place language between me and the ground. I will pave my way by constantly describing what's before me, so that it's my own description of it that I touch when I must touch the world.

It must be that I'm walking now to be saying so much about my feet. I am not walking, but talking has come to be like walking since I have started to use language as a kind of pavement. I move about on it. I move myself by way of it. Sometimes I slide across it and bump into things I didn't know were there. I bump into the empty space beyond it and pull out — a crustacean. The woman, now she notices me. I have been standing here watching her eat. The flesh of the crustacean is white and flakey. The flesh of the crustacean is nothing like my feet.

They are smooth. They manufacture their gloss while I sleep. They do not make gurgling sounds like babies do when they eat, but they are soft.

When I touch my feet with my hands, I feel my hands, not my feet. I do not feel "my feet are touching my hands," and I do not feel "my hands are touching my feet." I feel, "my hands are touching my hands." I feel, "I have no feet."

CASSIDY

At night the air waits for Cassidy the way it does for a fuse to free
its load. Then the great burst air gets to be, the blues and pinks
and falling greens of fleurs-de-lis the stars might have made when
stars were as young as Cassidy.

Coming along the path, Cassidy looks like he's falling toward
what's stopping me: the screen in the door that keeps bugs between us —

though something's eating through the screen —

but what looks like Cassidy is only a streak in the grass, Cassidy's path through the grass and trees. Though the path seems to be standing in the grass and the grass to be in the trees. And between the trees is a place that is always exchanging possibilities.

(Once in that place I found Cassidy. The air felt quicker before he knew I was watching. He was building something backwards, faster and faster. Digging a hole in his white t-shirt to bury everything in. I felt myself going in with everything, becoming the rounded tip of the planet. Before he knew I was watching, I wasn't other than the air; I was everywhere.)

.

How young is Cassidy? When ice on the lake breaks in spring, when anything breaks in spring, Cassidy is released from something green that I know has been waiting for me, and it is a fear-feeling, and it floats in the dust in the mirror after I haven't eaten breakfast again.

I know I will have been too slow; I know I will arrive after the side has been swiped; I know I will not be able to lift the weight off of Cassidy's cooling body.

These are fears that find different ways to me: sometimes it is just a cup I've lifted that brings me to a hole where I'm kneeling to see Cassidy.

Or a piece of paper I've forgotten to mail flaps like a carcass.

Or a pallor descends from ceiling to floor, brushing me.

Or looking through the screen I see an opening that used to be Cassidy; I see a bee sucking the opening; I see a swarm of openings forming a single thing that Cassidy used to be. (They keep their hive in a hollow tree. Their hum swallows me.)

.

Even gone, he gives off too many images — mist because the dew has to have its sunrise, the patchy flesh of the animal revived by what Cassidy would bring: Cassidy, but brought to me as if a thing to drink and be drunk off of, to wake up from with the feeling that whole lives of mine are missing — people I might have been had I not met him, people I might have met had he not been. Had Cassidy never met me, the mountains where my grandfather grew clutches of weeds for his family might have been flattened beneath some other family's feet.

Combined with his, my life's not mine — evidence of this is easy to find in drawers not often looked in: those aren't my clothes, and they aren't his; who is it then who lives?

I think I hear this other person sometimes.

I watch a woman where a window comes to drink.

I taste a surrounding mouth with mine.

At night, I am parted by the sides of something — something comes to drink from the birds that rustle softly in my chest.

In the gaps between my teeth, I see tiny other teeth.

I hear them blink. I let them eat.

Following the path Cassidy made through the grass to me, I come to my door. Through the screen I see what he would see behind me as I came toward the door: another door, another Cassidy raking his teeth across the screen.

The bedroom window opens me to so many bodies.

I sleep naked so that my teeth can see.

They are attracted by my warmth. They slip under and in. They double in my skin.

Other hair grows alongside mine; there's a new ring of blue circling my green eyes. I put my arms through holes made by moths and find the shirt fits me fine.

.

My other size is usually much too big for me, so fear comes to fill it with everything I can see about how little it all has to do with me. It is a house that fear makes for me; it is a door with a chewed-through screen; it is Cassidy coming back along the path that stands in the trees and screams.

He is carrying something heavy.

I let him lay her in my bed, her head where my feet would be. Her feet are very clean, but her bare head appears to have been walking for a long time. There are leaves and dirt in her hair, and they fall onto the sheet. When she asks for a glass of water, I bring her the one I drink from.

Cassidy has gone outside to leave. He isn't gone yet.

Where the path enters the trees, where light enters and leaves, his white shirt comes back for something I can't reach.

DISCOMFORT

While I am talking with him I am also walking, and I've lost track of where I am by the time our conversation pauses. Curtains get in the way, obstructing light as clutter obstructs movement. He is not someone I have ever been comfortable with — I can't recall his name — so I am more aware of my body while I'm walking and intonation while I'm talking than I am when with a familiar person, whose ways of judging me won't surprise me. It doesn't help that he's a back-patter and an arm-grabber, likes to touch while conversing. The wind, when it lifted and filled the curtains my mother hung in my bedroom, caused the curtains to take on the proportions of a body. When I am with him I take on his mood and bearing, which I don't generally do with anyone anymore, not since I was a child and an excellent mimic because shy and easily frightened. He tells me that we should see the exhibit he's so excited to see and has been talking about while we've been walking away from the building where I should have turned right, gone three blocks, and entered my apartment building. I like to eat meals alone and know I will be hungry at the exhibit because hunger, for me, is what happens when concentration lapses and becomes boredom. He will not yet be hungry because absorbed in his surroundings, so I will pretend not to be hungry.

I have finally arranged my apartment in a way that I like — sun on uncluttered surfaces, and blinds, no curtains. After I threw out all the things my mother had in storage, I bought the sort of table I've long admired but never purchased. Now I have the sort of table I admire, purchased from a furniture store near the printing shop where my father worked until his early death. The shop is still there, but it is owned by different people, not the two brothers who were identical in their rough treatment of me, so that they seemed to be the same person. I feared their language and mannerisms but not their bodies, whose names I could never remember, so I couldn't loathe them, because I might call one by the name of the one who was absent and thus not treating me in a way — patting my back, lifting me over his head, twirling me in circles and setting me down when I was dizzy — that made me nervous and uncertain. I rarely saw them together, so I came to think of them as one person. Of course I realized it was the wind and not really a person, but the likeness was uncanny, wind being an excellent mimic, in sound and movement, of human distress. Though I once pretended to be near-sighted, groping my way along blindly, I now wear glasses. The table is used, but the wood has been treated well, and its surface glows when sun fans across it through the blinds I keep open should something beautiful or unexpected happen outside my window, which looks out on the brick wall of the neighboring building — should the brick wall crumble, that I might see it.

The exhibit doesn't pertain to my interests, but I agree to go. Then I anticipate trying to find my way back to my building, where I look forward to eating a meal alone, facing the window and the brick wall beyond it, a meal that I purchased to celebrate something that is probably important to no one but me, so I don't mention it to the man after we agree to see the exhibit, and then our conversation pauses while we continue walking. I want him to part from me so that I can turn around and go back to my apartment. I liked the way my dresses belled out from my body when I was spun, but I hated having to stumble in circles, watched and laughed at, after. I'm too uncomfortable with him to mention that we've passed my turn, and I'm beginning to hope he doesn't ask me where I'm living. Telling him where I'm living would be like admitting that I've let him lead me away from my turn, that I've given him this power, and that now I will have to do more work to get where I am going than he will to get where he is going. I like to eat alone, though this can be difficult in practice. As a child I was often reminded that one cannot exist in a vacuum. Feeling my way along blindly, I wanted to find an unexpected doorway the size of my body. But then I realize I don't know where he's going, and I don't know where he lives.

Perhaps he was lost before we met on the street outside the market where I purchased the meal I anticipate eating alone, and he approached me because I am familiar, having a place in the structure of his memory. Like a body, only less reliably constant in proportion. The dampness had caused many of the boxes to become sodden, their contents mildewed, pages of books and letters and other handwritten documents illegible. Sorting through all of my mother's belongings took me weeks. Working alone in her dingy basement where light was scarce and dampness pervasive, I often became confused about where I was in the process, about which items I had decided to discard and about which I was uncertain. Stumbling, wanting badly to grab onto the first solid shape I came to for support. Clumsily, I shuffled together papers, photos and files, and as if a strong wind had blown across everything, any order that may have been there, and which may have told me something I didn't know about my mother, such as how she ordered her memories, was lost. I became lost easily as a child, losing myself in places I knew well, like the hallways of the elementary

school building, when anything about the places — light, wall dec-
orations, crowdedness — changed, and in conversations. For this
reason and probably others, I resisted change as if it were death.
But while one order was lost, a new one was created, one that
might have told me more about myself had I looked at it with dis-
cernment. Once I grabbed a man who I thought was my father
and was roughly shaken off, as if being given a lesson.

I'm not sure why I waited until after my mother's death to purchase the table. I remember I felt certain that he was my father —
the proportions were right — but rightness is a matter of conviction, which is often based on misunderstanding or at least near-
sighted apprehension. As I walked to the furniture store to choose
the table, I felt that today is the day, and now I will do it, buy the
thing I've long wanted but deny myself because I feel my stay here
is temporary, of insubstantial time. The doorway was the fantasy
of a child, but I still look for it when I am lost or lonely, and sometimes I see a structure or shadow and for a moment believe that I
have found it, that I will enter, that I will become something different. A curtain shifting before closed windows. My mother preferred curtains, but when arranging my apartment I have chosen
blinds because I never liked curtains. As a child I felt they were
concealing bodies in their folds, the bodies of judgmental people
who would follow me without retreat until I was old, and who
one day would carry me away like wind carries away leaves of paper. Finally my father would pick me up and carry me away from

discomfort. A conversation in which I'm ill at ease and lost finally pauses.

Finding the doorway made to fit only my body, I would enter and thereby escape the present situation. In a situation over which I have no control, I try to fit my preferences to those of others, and so will always be in many ways a child who is often lost and hungry. He likes to talk about his work, now I remember this about him. The exhibit will include something by him, he says, and though he is critical of some of the work that will appear near his, overall, he says, he thinks it will be a good show, well-organized, a good opportunity to network. I didn't like being the center of their attention and wished to hide behind a curtain. I feel the food I've purchased for my anticipated solitary meal losing heat, and this loss seems to come from my body. The exhibit, he begins his every sentence, the exhibit is ... If not a child, then a receptacle for others' thoughts and emotions.

Frustrated, I threw away all of the damp boxes. It has begun to rain, and I fear the food I've purchased will be soggy by the time I finally find my way to my apartment. One box contained a ceramic sculpture I made as a child of my head. My mother kept it though it was not good, showed no talent, and made my face look large and irregular where in life it isn't. Perhaps she enjoyed that about it, how exaggeration of the familiar can cause pleasant discomfort, such as laughter. I threw it out with the rest of her things, and afterward felt light, as if some weight had been lifted from my shoulders. I don't remember much about my childhood besides moments of discomfort.

I would get up to close the window and find it was closed and locked tight as a vacuum. The trails of ink along the walls of our house came from my father's hands between his arrival home from work and when he went to the sink in the basement, a pause mediated by distance and usually silence. He didn't operate the printing machines, the machines were operated by men whose faces were always red and thrown back in laughter at jokes my mother called off-color. The machines were loud, with many tubes and wires, and many dials and buttons, none of which, when I examined them, were clearly labeled. So I came to think of them as one person. Sometimes my father would have to touch them, and his hands would be stained. My mother and father were rarely in the same room together, even while sleeping. I'm not sure I ever saw them touch one another on purpose. Our walls were off-white and absorbent, showing paths my father's hands had taken, which distressed my mother because the ink was so apparent, and what would it say about us, and so on.

She kept saying that one day she would paint the walls a deep crimson or purple, maybe aubergine. My mother was a librarian and had stories about the words and stains she would find in margins

of returned books. She said she found an odd note, written in loop-
ing handwriting, in a book about a condition that causes those af-
flicted to read and write letters and words backwards. If I can claim
that a sense of direction is like the ability to read, then I will say
that I have written my path through this city in a way that I cannot now decipher. Or perhaps it is a problem of memory. Once I
entered the door, I would not be able to pass back through it. Par-
tial entry was not permitted. No backpedaling. After I threw away
all my mother's belongings, I considered that because she was a
librarian, she had likely put them in a specific order, possibly one
that would be unique and telling.

I have certain preferences pertaining to ink: I don't like it to smear
or run or bleed through the paper. Finally the pause is interrupted
when he asks me to write my telephone number on a small card he
hands me so that he can call me about going to the exhibit. It is his
calling card, and I see that his address is the building we're standing
outside of, the doorway large and overarching. My understanding
of such doorways is that they're meant to be intimidating, suggesting the smallness of the one entering compared with the largesse
of the overall structure. I am both relieved and aggravated that
he has not invited me in, and as I'm writing my phone number,
the rain causes the ink to run though we're standing beneath an
awning — the rain is running off my hand and onto the letters I'm
writing — the ink being the kind that bleeds and runs away. My
handwriting is often difficult to decipher, and sometimes I make

it difficult on purpose, to hide or obstruct the information contained there. You cannot always be alone, aren't you lonely, and other questions asked of me by my mother. She didn't want the walls to look like a bruise, she eventually decided, so she didn't paint them.

Because I was unable to carry the table to my apartment, a man at the furniture store strapped it to the bed of his truck and drove both me and the table the twelve or so blocks to my apartment. With furniture, it's just the surface you have to be careful of, but with people, unless it's a dead person's body, in which case it's more like furniture, there are all these invisible little things that can set them off, the little things related to bigger things, the big things like filters or warped glasses through which people perceive themselves and their surroundings. This, though not exactly, is what the man told me as we were driving, and while I thought the comparison between furniture and people was simple, I understood what he meant, that a person's past experience alters how she perceives her present surroundings, whereas the experience of furniture is recorded primarily on its surface. Along the way, the man got lost while telling me about how much he enjoyed the job at the furniture shop after working for so many years as a driver, first of a limo, then of a hearse. I did consider and fear when choosing it that its structure was compromised in ways that would only be apparent later, when I wasn't expecting it, though this has not happened yet as far as I am aware.

As I am writing my phone number and watching the just-inked numbers blur, he calls the work of another sculptor superficial, which is a word I don't like, because who's to say that what's beneath a surface is not another surface, that one is better than another? I liked to trace the ink marks on the off-white walls with my finger the way I liked to trace my parents' signatures, mimicking the loops and folds of their thoughts as they were writing, as if what's written is any indication of what the writer was thinking. When I knew him best was when I was in school, studying painting, and he was an assistant professor who let it be known that painting, while often subtle, is inferior to sculpture because it lacks a dimension, but I never knew him well, and didn't want to. This seemed like such a simple criticism, yet one he held to with conviction, and it became part of his reputation, which surrounded him like a vacuum. Other words that are similar to *simple*, and which I know I've used, perhaps unfairly: *facile, surface, superficial*.

Finally we part, he going into his building, me turning in a circle before setting out in a direction. Realizing that I was being watched and possibly mocked, I would press my skirt down though the feeling of baring my legs was alluring. I look into doorways for the comfort of seeing someone in the midst of entering or exiting, the door opening, the air of inside and outside exchanging, a mouth slightly open as if awaiting an answer or arriving at the beginning or end of a sentence, and I suppose I do this because

I would like to be where they are, in their thoughts for a moment. I tipped the man and thanked him for moving my table, which I could not have done alone, and he said something that concluded what he'd started to say earlier but left hanging — pink faded gum in the corner of his mouth — while he negotiated parking in a too-small space by pulling forward and backward, over and over, pivoting the steering wheel about his palm, motions that make me think of the tortuous movement — false starts, circling, backpedaling — that goes on in me while I negotiate difficult conversations, and often while I'm writing, which is like having a conversation with one's memory.

People want to give you directions, said the man helping me with my table, they want you to listen to their problems and do for them what they can't do for themselves, which is different for everyone, we all have different strengths and weaknesses, you might be able to do something I can't, but I can do something your neighbor can't, so power among people is constantly shifting, and I can't understand how any one person ever gets to a place of importance, though ignorance is rampant, and —

I make my way back to my apartment by asking for directions at every corner, a practice I would probably not like in another person, but now that I am lost and in need of direction so that I can go to my apartment and eat the meal that by now is cold and probably hardened where it isn't soggy, I forget about what I dislike in other people, so I feel like a stranger to myself. The bag of food has become heavy because sodden with rain water, but probably most of the heaviness comes from fatigue in my muscles. I can't now remember all of what the man said while he drove me and my table to my apartment, or how he said it, but it was something about nobody being alone, or all of us having to work together, the sort of thing I would not say aloud because I fear it would sound facile, though sometimes I think it and say it to myself, as if I'm trying to persuade a multitude that traces circles in dirt with its toes while it listens.

The doorway to my building is stuck open, as it always is, by a doorjamb fashioned out of a folded and faded cigarette box. Inside my apartment, I strip off my sodden clothing. My style of clothing might be called makeshift. Same with my style of decorating, except for the table, a concession to a growing sense that I am stuck corporeally — I don't believe in a soul or afterlife or the supernatural — moving in one direction, my past decisions providing unseen momentum that will eventually carry me away from everything familiar. The curtains that billowed across my closed window were likely moved by the air vent in the ceiling above them, or some other reasonable explanation. The next thing I do is I take containers of food out of the bag that is now falling apart, disintegrating in strips and pieces, and I set the containers out on the table, seeing that the mark the clerk made on each container as to its contents has bled and faded, thinking of my mother, who was very difficult to get along with in old age because she thought I was someone else, a person she called by different names, sometimes the name of someone she loathed, sometimes my name, which marks me as someone. On an uncluttered surface, I set out my meal. I do all of this while naked.

THE MONK AND THE NUN

According to the monk who has stayed in the same place for forty years, there is a nun who has also stayed in the same place for forty years, and like the monk, for forty years she has been examining the ways her mind forms attachments to its ideas and images, which she calls her self. The monk says that from where he has stayed for the past forty years, he can see the small hut where the nun has stayed, and the nun, when she comes out of her hut and looks a bit farther up the mountain, can see the monk's hut. So it seems that one of the things I have been examining, says the monk, is my attachment to seeing the nun's hut, and to seeing the nun come out and look up. I know that one day the nun will not come out of her hut, and soon after that day, the wind will have blown her hut to rubble, and rain will have washed the rubble down the mountain. The monk says that when he finds himself looking forward to seeing the nun's hut and the nun, he thinks about the hut being reduced one day to rubble, and the rubble being pulled slowly and inevitably down to the base of the mountain, where the monk's hut will also one day collect. And, the monk says, I have little doubt that the nun is similarly examining her mind's attachments to seeing my hut, for she will also know, being as devoted as she is to careful and honest examination of all her mind's fabrications, that my hut is bound in time to be reduced to rubble, just as hers is.

But it happened once, says the monk, that several days passed without the nun emerging from her hut, and my mind, being less disciplined than it is now, began spinning story after story about how the nun had died, or was lying gravely ill inside her hut. Having made a hut in his mind for the nun, a hut that was just as real to the monk as the nun's actual hut from which she had not emerged for several days, the monk could not tolerate a discrepancy between the nun's hut in his mind and the nun's actual hut, so he gathered a small bag of supplies for a day away from his hut and hastily began walking down the rocky path toward the nun's actual hut, the nun's hut in his mind having no path along which the monk might walk to access it.

When I came to the nun's hut, the monk says, I stood a distance from her doorway so that I might consider whether I really should enter it. Seeing that nothing would block my way, that the doorway was not barred, and no curtain obscured the hut's interior from my gaze, I decided that it was the same to gaze as it was to enter, so I began walking toward the doorway of her hut.

While he was paused in the doorway to allow his eyes to adjust to the dark interior, he tried to detect an odor of the nun, perhaps what she had recently eaten, or what she had rubbed on her skin to protect it from the sun. But he could not smell anything except the hut — an odor of dust and mountain.

When my eyes had adjusted and I could see the far wall of the nun's hut, which really wasn't so far from where I stood as the hut was quite small, says the monk, I entered and saw that the hut was empty. There was no sign of the nun or any sign that she had recently been there. There were no clothes, there were no strands of hair. No bits of food, no books containing words of insight. There was nothing except bare walls and bare floor, so I had to conclude that the nun had not been there for a very long time.

Nevertheless, says the monk, the next morning I saw the nun emerge from her hut carrying her bucket, and I watched her set off down the path toward the stream where she fills her bucket with water. A bit later I saw her coming back along the path carrying her bucket, which was now full of water, and which she carried into her hut. And that evening I saw her emerge with the same bucket and set off again down the path toward water. And every morning and evening since then, I have watched the nun emerge from her hut carrying her bucket. And so it seems I have formed quite a powerful attachment to the nun and her comings and goings, and though I sit all day and most of each night in silence so that I can accurately perceive the workings of my mind, all of the images and ideas it clings to as if these were as real as the mountain on which I sit, something among them has so far eluded me, and I can no longer see any difference between the nun's hut in my mind and the nun's actual hut, which I suspect by now is rubble at the base of the mountain.

BLONDLOT'S TRANSFORMATION

In Nancy, Blondlot is missing and police are investigating trees.

"They're so shadowy," says the chief. "See?"

We're looking at oaks in the chief's back yard.

"Do you know," he says, "that trees *breathe*?"

I've been called to see what the chief sees — arrows among the leaves, a sort of directionality. Blondlot, guiding our eyes?

"*That's* Blondlot," says the chief.

"Where?"

"The way those sparrows are arranged."

.

The requirements of my work are these: I must not fear what I might see. I must look with honesty at rugs that are ugly; I must not turn away out of boredom from a placid lake — at any moment its surface may break and there will be the beast I have been hired to see. I must be patient; I must not let my clients' eyes or desires become mine. I must never doubt my ability to see things only as they are, not as my client wants them to be.

My clientele have changed during the many years that I have been — officially — a notary. At one time I was hired to witness acts of magic — witches said to levitate, a leviathan inhabiting a lake. At times farther back in the past, I was invited to divine the future from handfuls of animals' intestines flung onto ceremonial grass. Now I am employed by a science magazine to examine the apparatuses of dubious inquiries. There are also business people in windowless boardrooms who ask that I assess presentations before they are delivered to important clients. Occasionally I am contacted by a man who seems utterly ordinary, except that when I am sitting in his living room, he repeats, "Anything missing? Do you see anything that's missing?" This poor man who lives alone suspects himself of thievery.

By license I am a notary, yet my ability to see, observe, witness has something in it that surpasses me. I receive requests from all over the world to come and see what can't be seen, or what can be seen but can't be believed. And so I go, feeling that I am being led by a confidence I do not possess yet that travels with me, within me, and that does not subside when my body and mind are tired.

·

In the stripes of my tie, the chief sees possibilities for a ladder that extends between different states of matter — one can climb from a solid to a liquid, a liquid to a gas, a gas back to liquid, and finally down to solid ground.

Such a ladder, the chief says, will provide a tether to the soul, the most gaseous form of matter, the most difficult to control.

I suggest the complexities of anchoring such a ladder; he shows me his drawing: a ladder extends from a stick man into a tree, from the tree to nearby nebulae, from these to a dark gray haze beyond the Milky Way.

The range of our investigation has widened beyond my ability to believe.

·

As a child I imagined myself the setting of all that would happen to me — a theater with its curtain raised, its empty stage awaiting the entrance of actors and audience and the lively tension between them that would constitute my inner life. Yet nothing ever became of that stage, or rather it is still empty, its curtain still raised; and all that I thought would happen inside of me has happened outside, in light that does not dim or brighten according to a score. My inner life has happened out where anyone can stumble into it, and I have had to watch the effects of this on my chances at romance — I imagine a sudden catastrophe befalling the man sitting across from me, something poisonous about his dinner, and then this poor fellow's face is gray and he cannot breathe.

Any kind of interiority, a private place where I can perform my fantasies, has so far eluded me, and now, when I try to see in my mind the stage I awaited as a child, its wings reaching into the distant domains I wanted my interior to contain, I only see the dimensions and effects of my hotel room in Nancy, its bed, desk, chair; its single window, and through it, the brick of a neighboring building.

.

I'm in Blondlot's tidy entryway where his shoes go in rows, his coats hang around their empty insides, and inside one pocket there's a list of Christmas gifts — everything exed except the words *not those*.

"Why can't something that isn't really there be a man who once wore striped underwear?" Through the living room window the chief is watching trees that appear to be trees.

Blondlot's wife shows me everything Blondlot would wear — to prove he packed no bag before he disappeared.

"What might he buy that would be new," I ask her, "like a disguise?"

She brings her hands to cover her eyes. "He liked to carve wooden things in the evenings," she says, "little men, little guys."

·

I start seeing their likenesses in everyone I meet in Nancy.

At the cafe, I admire truckers' hands twisting the thick uppers they're unwrapping and swallowing with coffee. I think of Blondlot making these men — how would he have held each one as he lathed his veins?

From some faces, Blondlot has omitted lips; from others, chins are missing. Even in the chief, in the wrinkles around his eyes, I see Blondlot's tool for carving fine lines.

At the mall, there are some faces that convey nothing at all: these interest me most because in them I can find nothing of who Blondlot might have been. No residue of the thoughts he might have had as he shaped their blank foreheads — yet it's possible that these empty faces have the most to teach me about Blondlot's disappearance.

But at the mall, there are too many reflections of me; they interfere with my investigations of others. Surfaces are cleaned frequently by the bored clerk — they reflect light precisely — and I find I'm greeting my own reflection with the mild smile I show strangers, concealing my teeth as a sign of passivity. In public I appear to be always swallowing.

Soon I am too self-conscious to see anything but my own anxieties in the faces around me. A man dabs a fragrance on my pulse and his touch is so tactful, so utterly unlike my attitude toward myself, I feel he has mistaken me for somebody else. I apologize but then I see — he is only trying to sell me this bottle of Bandit.

·

A mind makes all sorts of fantastic species out of the facts — the shadow cast by a woman's body on the floor becomes a measure of her distance above it; flickering bodies of fishes fuse into a single, sinuous existence the mind makes a monster.

Times when I've attended closely to my experience, I've found that the texture I ordinarily take for contiguous is in fact a series of consecutive moments of awareness separated by gaps — concavities, some quite large, others finer than the smallest increment on a jeweler's ruler — from which my awareness is wholly absent, and wherein must lurk the leviathans of my superstitions, those creatures whose persistence depends on their never being fully seen.

Back in my hotel room, I attempt to manufacture absences using the pattern in the carpet — try to see darker shades recede, creating a lower realm above which vault the brighter aspects of the pattern. Within that lower realm I try to see myself and the chief — though he has a wife and I am a man of integrity, I still want to know what it would be like to lie with him beneath a cartogram of yellow sunbursts and purple spirals.

But I cannot make sufficient depth out of the pattern; I only manage to make a blur of things until morning.

·

This evening I am on the lake with the chief. We've motored out here because he wants me to see Blondlot rise from the trees, an event he says has been happening nightly in Nancy since Blondlot's disappearance.

"Do you mean," I ask, "evaporation — steam?"

The chief encourages me to say *transformation* — nightly in Nancy since Blondlot's *transformation*.

I emend the official record, what little there is.

·

From the hotel I follow the sluice that flows through Nancy.

I used to believe that if I could learn to look at things differently, a different world would be visible to me, or a variation on this one would present its familiar aspects so strangely, I would have to learn anew who I am.

I would try to blink more frequently, believing that even a small alteration at the surface of my eye would drastically change things — by some kind of echo effect, or the way a pebble's size is magnified by the surface it interrupts.

But those were habits of a child (though I depended on them well into middle age). I am less hopeful now that the world maintains a secret sea, a private beach where this world's washed-up waste is smoothed into new use.

Yet sometimes I do sense a presence inside or behind the thing I see that is more real than the thing I see. It lives just beyond visibility and gives the visible its energy. In any case I feel this way about the swans in Nancy — that theirs is a form this invisible vitality is comfortable inhabiting, and which it uses to build its nests out of the garbage that accumulates in the sluice.

·

Tomorrow the investigation ends officially. In the morning I'll meet the chief and Blondlot's wife for coffee and consolations; tonight I go alone by cab to the Funhouse, the club where, a few evenings ago, Blondlot and I arranged to meet.

I had been sitting in one of those lounges I sometimes come to in Nancy when the street I've been following turns out not to be the street I thought I'd been following, and instead of walking into the bright entryway of the hotel, I am in a dim stairwell, searching for my identification so as to enter a nameless place.

It turns out that the disparity between a place and its representation is a lounge where everyone tries to have an experience they've had somewhere else. I was sitting by myself, having the experience of sitting by myself, when a woman I recognized sat next to me.

I recognized the woman from the photograph of Blondlot the chief keeps in his case log.

The feeling of recognition I recognized, too — it came from a time when I was a child and out for a walk in the city with my father. Idly I had glanced into an open basement window and there saw a small room where several men were surrounded up to their necks in cut flowers. The men were not smiling; the flowers were of many kinds and colors, and it was as if the men were drowning in them. Though I had seen men before, and flowers, and a room like the small wood-paneled one whose window I looked through, I was so startled by the uncanny assemblage of familiar elements that I fell immediately asleep. When I later woke in my own bedroom, the recollection of that other room cast into my room a marvelous little band of light the color of heliotrope as impalpable as a reflection and laid down like a carpet of petals over which I did not tire of walking back and forth with lingering, nostalgic steps.

Blondlot wore a dress the color of which I have forgotten, if I ever knew, or else, remembering that evening when I had woken in my own room, I saw the band of heliotrope enveloping Blondlot as he sat beside me, and I never did notice the actual color of the dress he was wearing. In the notebook I have carried since beginning Blondlot's case I at some point in the night drew a question mark next to the word *dress* in script that does not resemble my usual one: the question mark looks like a bubble, with little lines dimpling it that show its tautness.

Blondlot and I talked, he saying nothing of his recent transformation and I saying nothing of it, either. The next day, which was yesterday, the chief and I carried on our investigation, I saying nothing about having spent the night with Blondlot.

Tonight I'm dressed in the only suit I brought with me to Nancy — a tailored black Armani with tricot trousers and a front vest that closely fits my *slim physique* — those words only occur to me when I am wearing this vest. I had anticipated a funeral, or some other somber ceremony to conclude our investigation, but tonight, dressed as I am, I find myself wanting to dance holding a neon-bright drink in one hand, Blondlot in the other.

.

I pay my drivers well, always. Maybe because my vest fits me better than I'd remembered it fitting, tonight I give an extra twenty.

"Where am I?" I ask, handing him the money.

"Thanks very much," he says.

I'm wondering where I am, yet it's easy to see trees and moonlight — in my present mood they make gauzy scrims out of distance, and as I walk up the driveway to the Funhouse, I'm waving my arms in front of my face, warding off the impression of special effects intended to build suspense.

.

Nobody knows what energy *is*, Blondlot is saying. We are in a room where the floor comes unexpectedly at one's feet, suggesting that the corners of the room are not in the room but somewhere far outside of it.

Blondlot describes research he had been doing before his disappearance — his laboratory is well known in Nancy because of

Blondlot's famous discovery, the N-ray, which other scientists have demonstrated cannot exist.

I know that back in my hotel room I'll see, in the white wrinkles and folds of my sheets, the way Blondlot's dress gathered and carried him from one gesture to the next, so that Blondlot's thoughts seemed to belong to the dress which nodded no and yes and fidgeted Blondlot's hands. I'll see how I had questioned the dress about Blondlot's disappearance — transformation? — and how the dress had excused Blondlot and lifted him slowly from the table, carrying him, within its perfect conformity to his body, to a place where I couldn't see him, then returning him to my table, where I repeated my question.

Later, my relief at seeing stars in their familiar positions; my ride in the taxi alone to my hotel room, where I see all of this in the white sheets of my unmade bed — I had asked housekeeping for no disturbance.

.

While Blondlot talks, the flame of a candle gutters between us, and I can hear it — it makes a sound like a car traveling along a bumpy road as its light disappears and reappears, as if I'm watching it through trees, my departure already seen.

I might write in my notebook, *When there is real distance between us, what will Blondlot be?* Because I am beginning to have the sense that Blondlot's appearance is because of me — his dress is still the color I see when I remember that afternoon in my bedroom, how I had marveled at the way a simple band of sunlight, reflected by the neighboring house's curtained window, could become a passageway to a place I would likely not see again.

I close my eyes, and when they are open again, Blondlot has stopped talking. He has moved off to a corner and laughs as I try to navigate my legs — they cannot find the proper ways to bend in relation to the situation we're in.

Yet, by some mechanism — I credit my patience — I eventually reach him, and my fantasy of dancing with a cocktail in one hand and Blondlot in the other becomes my present circumstance: by some mechanism. I hope never to discover it. Its mystery I already miss.

ACKNOWLEDGEMENTS

Black Warrior Review (Blondlot's Transformation, winner of the 2012 fiction contest), BOMB (Mole), *Brooklyn Rail* (Girl), *The Collagist* (Nowhere Hill, winner of the 2010 nonfiction contest), *Web Conjunctions* (Julian), *Denver Quarterly* (Interruptions), *Everyday Genius* (The Largest Unobstructed Area Given to Ham), *Flyway* (Office, runner up in the 2011 "Notes from the field" contest), *Harp & Altar* (Discomfort), *Hobart* (Cassidy), LIT (My Chute), MINIMAL BOOKS (Polish translations of Interruptions and The Fox and the Wolf), *Mothers News* (The Monk and the Nun), *New York Tyrant* (Boy), *Sidebrow* (EEG), *Unsaid* (The Fox and the Wolf, published in *Unsaid* with the title "Stories of the Things That Had No Power of Their Own")

EVELYN HAMPTON lives in California. She is the author of the chapbook *We Were Eternal and Gigantic* (Magic Helicopter Press).

ellipsis

• • •

press